Last Hope

A Last Healer Mystery

By Charles Huss

ISBN: 979-8-9991948-2-4

For my mom, Nancy, who is not only a great mom but also a great proofreader. I usually wait until the seventh or eighth draft, when I know I caught all my mistakes, and then let her read my book before anyone else. She then sends me a list of corrections.

Chapter 1

Grace Ellington walked hand in hand with her date towards the front steps of her home. The weather was unseasonably mild for early January in Wisconsin, cold enough to need a jacket but warm enough that she left it unzipped over her pink sweater and black skirt. She stopped a few feet short of the steps, turned to her date, and took his hands. "Thanks for a lovely evening. I really enjoyed seeing you again."

"It was great to see you again, too, Grace. When we went our separate ways after high school, I assumed that was the end. I figured some handsome college guy would snatch you up. I'll be honest, I've never stopped thinking about you."

"I've thought of you, too. I guess you never forget your first love."

"Would you like to invite me in?"

"Maybe another time. I had too much to drink, and you know how alcohol makes me tired. I want to go straight to bed."

They kissed goodnight. It began as a soft, tender kiss that quickly turned passionate. The man reached his hand under Grace's sweater, causing her to pull back.

"What are you doing? Stop!" she protested.

"Oh, Come on, Grace! I know you. Don't pretend you don't want it."

"I'm not pretending. I don't want it. I'm tired. Is sex the only reason you wanted to go out with me tonight? I should have known better. You haven't changed."

He held her hand and said, "I'm sorry. I didn't go out with you for sex. I really did miss our time together."

He pulled her close and kissed her again.

Graced backed away while he continued to hold her hand. "I think maybe you had a little too much to drink, too," she said.

He pulled her close again. "It's been years, Grace. I miss you. I can't wait another day."

Grace took a step back, but the man held her wrist. She tried to break his grip, but he squeezed tighter, causing her pain. This angered her, so she slapped his face, hoping he would let go of her. He didn't. Instead, he looked at her with rage in his eyes. She feared what would come next. Nothing happened for several seconds. Then he slapped her hard across the cheek.

The rest seemed to happen in slow motion. Grace felt the pain of the slap. The force knocked her off balance. She felt her body falling backward. She tried to hold the man's hand to stop her fall, but her fingers slipped through his. She thought about what her dad would do to him when he found out. Then she felt her head hit the concrete. It was the last thing she ever felt. The light in her eyes, which could always brighten a room, faded into darkness.

***

Detective David Barclay parked his car at the Minaka Marina and stepped out into the unusually mild air. A sudden breeze reminded him it was still winter. He zipped up his jacket and scanned the many finger docks that jutted out from the main dock. The marina was empty of boats. All had been removed for winter storage two months earlier or moved south to a more temperate area. Several people had gathered near the dock on the far right. That must be where he needed to go.

His mornings usually dragged. Paperwork occupied much of his time. The life of a small-town detective was not glamorous. It was far from what television shows portrayed, but today felt different.

He took out his badge and used it to part the people hovering nearby. He assumed they were workers from the nearby seafood restaurant, who decided this was more interesting than food prep. On the far side of the onlookers, two police officers stood preventing people from accessing the crime scene.

The older of the two was Sergeant Ken Daniels. He was in his early thirties, average height, with short, dark hair and a well-groomed mustache. He was a muscular man, but his friendly face and demeanor put people at ease.

The other officer was Cheryl Ripley. She was in her mid-twenties and had been with the police department for a little over six months. She

3

applied to the police academy after a brief stint in the Army, where she served as a military police officer. She could have been a model with her long auburn hair and perfect body, but she was too much of a tomboy for that. She could also be quite intimidating when she wanted to be.

David ducked under the yellow crime scene tape and greeted the two officers by their first names.

"Good morning, Dave," Ken said. "A hell of a way to start a morning, huh?"

"What do we have here?" Dave asked.

"A body floated into the marina sometime last night or early this morning," Ken said. "A security guard noticed it by the dock a little after sunrise as he was doing his rounds. He pulled it out of the water and called us."

"Are you sure it floated in? Maybe the person died here."

"That's possible," Ken said, "but the security guard said that when the river is higher than usual, like it is now due to the melting ice and snow, the marina tends to collect debris from the river."

"I wouldn't call a dead body 'debris.'" Dave said.

"I agree. I was repeating what he had told me."

"Do you know who it is?"

"It's Grace Ellington," Cheryl said.

"The mayor's daughter? Are you sure?"

"Yes. I know her well. I mean, I knew her well. I dated her brother in high school."

"Oh, shit! Does anyone else know yet?"

"We called the chief," Cheryl said.

"What a mess. I wouldn't want to be in the chief's shoes today. Okay, let's go see the body."

Ken looked at Cheryl and said, "Wait here and keep these people away."

The two men walked to the end of the dock where the body lay, covered by a sheet. Dave pulled the sheet down partway, revealing the corpse. Her once-blond hair was dirty and tangled. Her face was pale and bloated. Her lips were a bluish-purple, and her eyes were closed. Dave wondered if she died with them closed or if someone had closed them. It didn't matter much, especially to her.

He pulled the sheet down further, looking for wounds. He didn't see any.

"Do you think she drowned?" Ken asked.

"I don't know. Maybe. She's dressed like she spent the night out on the town. Maybe she was out on a date. I'm not sure what she would have been doing near the water, though."

"Maybe she and her date were up by the old lighthouse?"

"That's where teenagers go. I think she's a little old for that. Besides, if she were there and fell in, wouldn't her date have called 911?"

Ken scratched his head. "So, how do you think she ended up in the water?"

Dave pulled rubber gloves from his pocket and put them on. He turned the body over and noticed the wound on the back of her head. "This might have something to do with it."

5

"Damn! Maybe she fell in the water and hit her head on a rock or something," Ken said.

"Or someone hit her on the back of the head and threw her in the river."

Ken raised an eyebrow. "Murder? We haven't had a murder in this town in years."

"We can't know for sure until the medical examiner looks at the body, but murder seems likely. If it were murder, someone dumped her body in the river, probably hoping the current would carry her far away. They didn't anticipate she would drift into the marina."

"Is it true?" came a voice from behind the two men. They both turned to see the chief of police standing behind them.

At six feet four inches tall, Chief Tom Bronson was an imposing figure. He wore his formal police uniform under an unbuttoned coat. His hat was noticeably absent. A gust of wind ruffled his salt and pepper hair. "Is it really the mayor's daughter?"

"Cheryl confirmed it," Ken said.

"Damn! There are times when I hate this job. This is one of those times." He turned to Ken and said, "Tell Cheryl to come here. I want to be a hundred percent sure before I tell the mayor his daughter is dead."

"Sure thing, Chief," Ken said before walking away.

"Do you know how she ended up in the water?" the chief asked.

"Not yet," Dave said. He pointed to her head. "She has a wound on the back of her head. She either hit it when she fell in the water, or someone killed her and threw her in the river."

"Do you think someone murdered her?"

"I think the odds are better than fifty-fifty that someone did this to her."

The chief shook his head. "The mayor is going to be devastated. She was a smart young woman who never hurt anybody. Who would want her dead?"

"I don't know," Dave said as he turned the body back over. He looked her over for more clues and noticed her left hand was closed. He gently pried open her fingers. "Well, what do we have here?"

"What? What is it?" the chief asked.

Dave took an evidence bag from his pocket and placed the object in it. He held it up so the chief could see it. "It's a ring. A man's ring, from the look of it. It has a letter engraved on it."

Chief Bronson took the bag and examined the ring closely. "Maybe it's the first letter of the guy's name."

"Maybe. It could also be the first letter of a high school or college. If it is, we could probably match the typeface to the school."

The chief looked at the ring again for a long moment. "You have your work cut out for you on this one."

When Cheryl arrived, she said, "You wanted to see me, Chief?"

"Yes. I need to know for certain that this is Grace Ellington."

"I'm afraid so." She pointed to her right hand. "She has a birthmark on the back of her hand. Do you see it?"

Both men looked and noticed a mark the size of a pea on the back of Grace's hand. "It looks like I have to pay the mayor a visit," the chief said. "I am not looking forward to this."

When Dave left the marina, he drove north, looking for areas where someone could dump a body inconspicuously. He drove upriver but found no secluded place in town. He did find a dirt road leading to the river less than a quarter mile north of the town line. He got out and looked around. There were no houses or businesses in sight. He noticed fresh tire tracks on the dirt road but found no other evidence in the area.

When he returned to town, he parked behind the police station. As he walked toward the rear entrance, a man called out from behind him. It was a voice he recognized.

"You have a flat tire, Dave," the man said.

Dave turned and saw the man pointing at the rear passenger-side tire of his car. "Oh, shit!" he said. He returned to his car and saw the flat tire. "That's weird. I didn't notice it while I was driving."

"It must have just happened," the man said. "Open the trunk. I'll help you change it."

Dave opened the trunk and removed the jack. He slid it under the car and began jacking it up. The last thought to ever enter his mind was what a terrible day it turned out to be.

Chapter 2

Katie awoke at daybreak and reached over to touch Joe, but he wasn't there. She got up, stretched, and put on a robe. She padded into the kitchen, drawn by the smell of bacon and coffee. Joe stood by the stove cooking while young Joey sat at the table in his highchair, eating scrambled eggs with his fingers.

"Good morning, Honey," Joe said. "Breakfast will be ready soon."

Katie smiled and slid into the seat next to Joey while Joe poured her a cup of coffee, added cream, and set it on the table in front of her. She yawned and said, "You're too good to me."

"It's the least I can do after all the work you put in yesterday getting everything ready for Joey's birthday party."

"Who would have thought a one-year-old's birthday party would be so much work. He probably won't even remember it when he's older."

"Oh, he'll remember it because I plan on taking a lot of photos."

"You did a great job chronicling the lives of your other kids with photos. They were lucky to have a photographer for a dad. Most kids growing up in the forties and fifties didn't have that."

Joe finished cooking, placed scrambled eggs and bacon on two plates, and carried them to the dining table. He kissed Katie on the cheek and sat down next to her. Joey had stopped eating his eggs and was drinking juice from a sippy cup.

"You know, part of the reason I liked photography as a child is that it is a way to hold on to memories," Joe said. "I'm sure you never noticed, but I can be forgetful at times."

Katie had taken a bite of eggs and almost spat them out when she laughed. She wiped her mouth with a napkin and, still smiling, said, "You? Forgetful? I don't believe it."

"You can laugh, but we can't all be perfect."

Katie put her hand on Joe's and said, "I like that you're not perfect. I mean, you're perfect physically, but if you were perfect mentally, I would feel unneeded."

"Oh, I definitely need you."

They kissed. It was a soft, tender kiss that lingered until the sound of a plate hitting the floor brought them back to reality. They both looked at Joey, who was laughing.

"You think that's funny, huh?" Katie said, smiling at Joey.

Joey laughed again, and Katie picked him up and hugged him. "I guess you're done eating now."

Katie finished eating while holding Joey. She then changed his diaper while Joe cleaned the kitchen. After she cleaned Joey up and changed his clothes, she put him in his playpen while she and Joe got ready for the big day.

An hour later, they arrived at the Three Eagles Ski Resort. Susan was working at the front counter. She was Joe's daughter and the only surviving child from Joe's first marriage. She was in her early eighties but had the energy of someone much younger.

Two years earlier, when Joe learned he could use his healing powers to help others, not just himself, he brought his family to optimum health. What he didn't do was reverse the appearance of aging. Susan and her son, Michael, both agreed that looking younger would draw too much attention to the family. The last thing Joe wanted was to become a lab rat at a top-secret government facility. Even if the government left him alone, he would never find peace from the media or people seeking healing from one ailment or another.

"There's the birthday boy," Susan said as Katie put Joey down and removed his coat. She knelt and extended her arms. "Come here, Joey, and give me a hug."

Joey carefully walked to Susan. It was slow and deliberate. He wobbled a little but made it without falling. Susan hugged him. "That was so good, Joey. I bet you will be an athlete one day."

"Joey adores you, Susan," Katie said. "Would you mind watching him for a while? I have some work to do before the party."

"I'll watch the front counter," Joe said.

"It will be my pleasure to hang out with my little brother."

Ninety minutes later, Katie gave up trying to work. She shared an office with Michael, but when the resort's accountant arrived, she couldn't concentrate on her work, so she joined Joe at the reception desk. A little while later, Michael emerged from his office, followed by the accountant. He said, "We just finished our taxes, and profit is up over twenty percent from the year before."

"I think we can thank Katie for most of that," Joe said.

"I agree," Michael said. "I don't know what you are doing on the marketing end, Katie, but it's working."

The door opened, and Katie's parents walked in. Katie walked around to greet them. They hugged, and Katie said, "I'm so glad you could make it."

"Are you kidding?" her mom said. "We wouldn't miss our grandson's first birthday for the world." She looked Katie up and down and added, "Married life must be good for you. You look younger every time I see you."

Katie glanced at Joe, who winked at her. Joe made an exception for Katie, thinking she shouldn't look older than him.

"Where is little Joey, anyway?" Katie's mom asked.

"He's in the banquet room with my grandmother," Joe said.

Since Katie's parents were not aware of Joe's ability, it was easier to refer to Susan as his grandmother. According to the official records, Joe was Michael's adopted son, which technically made Susan his grandmother. The documents were altered years earlier by a computer hacker whom Joe had paid to change his identity.

Joe's father died during the First World War, and his mother died when Joe was born. He was given the name Josip Novak at birth to honor his mother's last request, but he became Joe Young several months later when he was adopted. The last time he changed his name, he went back to Josip Novak, but everyone still called him Joe.

They all went to the banquet room and found Susan sitting on a chair while little Joey admired the bow on one of his many gifts. When she saw Katie's parents, she stood and said, "Hello again. I haven't seen you two since the wedding. Let me see if I can remember. Mary and Konrad, right?"

"My name is Karl, but that was close." Katie's father said.

They shook hands, and Mary said, "It is nice to see you again, Susan. You look wonderful." She then turned to look at Joey, "Oh, look at him. He is so adorable."

Little Joey wore brown pants, tennis shoes, and a black shirt with "Daddy is older than Mommy" printed on it.

"Where did that shirt come from?" Joe asked, "He wasn't wearing that earlier."

"I might have bought it for him," Katie said, looking away.

"He fell and hurt his hand," Susan said. "I cleaned the wound and put a bandage on it, but he got blood on his shirt, so I changed it to one in his bag."

Katie knelt to look at Joey's hand. She pulled off the bandage and looked at the wound. "Look at this, Joe," she said.

Joe knelt next to her and looked at Joey's hand. The cut was barely visible, as if it had happened days ago. Joe looked at Katie and whispered, "It appears I am no longer the last Healer."

"How is that possible?" Katie whispered. "Don't both parents have to come from the village where your parents came from?"

"We always assumed that, but we don't know where my abilities come from. Besides, you once mentioned your great-grandmother was from Croatia. Maybe she was from that village, or somewhere near there."

"That's right," Katie said. "If she were from that village, it would be quite a coincidence."

"I have seen stranger coincidences in my lifetime," Joe said. He waved at Susan. When she came near, Joe showed her Joey's hand. "Did you know about this?"

Susan's eyes widened. "Oh, my! Joey is like you, Dad. That's wonderful."

"Now you have a young apprentice," Katie said, smiling.

"He will need someone who understands him," Joe said. "I wish I had that when I was growing up."

"What didn't you have growing up?" came Mary's voice from behind Susan. "I'm sorry. I didn't mean to eavesdrop. I just wanted to see if I could do anything to help."

"It's fine, Mom," Katie said. "Thanks, but everything is taken care of. We were talking about Joe's childhood."

"What didn't you have in your childhood, Joe?"

"Oh, uh, pictures. I don't have many pictures of me as a child."

"That's surprising considering you grew up in the age of digital photography."

Joe looked at Katie and then at Mary. "My parents were never into photography like I am."

Michael's son, Eric, and his wife, Rachel, entered the banquet room with their daughter, who was almost two years old. Right behind them was Katie's friend, Ashley, and her family. Everyone greeted the new arrivals, and Katie said. "We're just waiting for Jenna and her family, then we can get this party started."

"I'm surprised they aren't here yet," Joe said.

Katie looked at her watch. "Maybe they got held up. I'll call her."

She took out her phone and dialed Jenna's number. It rang four times and went to voicemail. She hung up before leaving a message. "That's strange."

"What's strange?" Joe asked.

"They should be in the car driving here. Why wouldn't she answer the phone?"

"I don't know. There could be a hundred reasons. I wouldn't worry about it."

"I guess you're right. She'll call me back when she sees I called."

Katie called Jenna twice more during the party, but she didn't answer. When the party was over, Katie sat alone, looking at her phone. Only she, Joe, and Katie's parents remained in the banquet room. Joe could see she was worried and said, "Staring at the phone isn't going to make her call you any sooner. Call her. Find out what happened."

"I've called her three times already."

"So? Call her four times."

"You're right. I will." Katie dialed Jenna's number. This time, she answered on the third ring.

"Hi, Katie. I'm so sorry we missed little Joey's party."

Katie put her phone on speaker and said, "It's okay. I'm here with Joe and my parents. Are you still coming?"

"I'm afraid not. Something terrible has happened."

Katie looked at Joe and her parents, concern on her face. She looked back at the phone. "What happened?"

"David Barclay was murdered," she said as she started to cry.

Katie's eyes widened in shock. "Oh, my God. I don't believe it."

"It gets worse," Jenna said and started crying again.

"Take a deep breath, Jenna. Tell me what happened."

After a few seconds, Jenna composed herself and said, "Mitch was arrested for his murder."

"What?" Katie blurted out. Everyone listening looked at each other in shock. "Mitch is a big teddy bear. He wouldn't hurt a soul."

"I know that, but they don't."

"Have you talked to Mitch? What's his side of the story?"

"I don't know. I'm at the jail now. They won't let me talk to him yet. I'm about to have a nervous breakdown."

"How are the kids handling it?"

"My parents are watching them now. We haven't told them much. Hell, we don't know anything."

"You hang in there. I need to talk to Joe. I'll call you back in five minutes."

Katie hung up and looked at Joe, "We need to help them. I know Mitch, and I promise you he would never do anything like this."

Joe nodded slowly and said, "Okay, but what about Joey?"

"We'll watch him," Mary offered. "I can't think of a better way for our grandson to get to know us. Besides, we're on vacation this week."

"That's right," Karl said. "You need to help your friend. If anyone can prove Mitch is innocent, it would be you two."

"You can stay at our house and we'll stay here at the resort," Mary said. "That way, you can concentrate on your work, and Joey can stay where he is comfortable."

Katie looked at Joe, who nodded. She looked back at her parents and said, "You guys are the best." She then hugged each of them.

She called Jenna back and told her they would be heading there shortly.

"I was hoping you would say that. The police won't investigate this as thoroughly as you and Joe will. Now that they think they have their man, they probably won't investigate it at all."

17

"It doesn't help that someone murdered their only detective," Katie added before realizing what she said.

Jenna started to cry again.

"I'm sorry, Jenna. Don't worry. We'll be there soon and get this all straightened out."

"No. Enjoy the rest of Joey's birthday. Until I learn what happened, there's nothing for you to do."

"Okay. We'll drive there tomorrow morning."

After Katie hung up, they all left the banquet room and found Joey with Susan. They were in the lobby near the front desk. Joey was sitting with Eric and Rachael's daughter, but they were both doing their own thing. "We have a bit of an emergency," Joe announced. "We'll be going to Katie's hometown in the morning. Mary and Karl will stay here and take care of Joey."

"What's the emergency?" Susan asked.

"It's my friend, Jenna," Katie said. "Her husband was arrested for murder. I'm certain he is innocent. We need to help him."

"That's terrible," Susan said. "If anyone could help, it would be you two. Don't worry about Joey. We'll all be here for backup."

"I appreciate that, Susan," Katie said.

"You two should go home and get a good night's sleep," Mary said. "We'll take care of Joey tonight."

Katie and Joe went home without Joey for the first time in recent memory. As they were packing for their trip, Joe said, "You know, your parents are good people. We should consider telling them about me."

"I agree, Joe. I want to tell them. I want you to keep them healthy like you do for your family and for me, but I feel guilty."

"You feel guilty? Why?"

"Because we didn't tell them right away. Now, every time I see them, I want to say something, but I worry they will be mad that we kept them in the dark for so long. If that's not bad enough, the longer we wait, the more I don't want to say anything."

Joe hugged Katie and said, "I'm sorry. It's my fault for discouraging you from saying anything in the first place."

"It's not your fault. You didn't know them back then."

"I know them now. When this case is over, we can tell them together, and I will tell them it was me who wanted to keep them in the dark."

"I appreciate the gesture, Joe, but I'm not going to lie to my parents."

When they finished packing, Katie said, "I can't remember the last time we were alone like this."

Joe took her in his arms and kissed her. "We shouldn't let an opportunity like this go to waste."

Katie smiled. "You have a one-track mind. Aren't you worried about Joey?"

"Yesterday, I would have been. I always felt I needed to be close to him in case he got hurt or sick. Now that I know he is like me, I don't need to worry so much."

"You have a good point," Katie said before kissing Joe passionately. She unbuttoned his shirt and removed it. She never saw Joe work out, except when doing physical labor around the house or at the resort, yet he was always in perfect shape.

Joe pulled off Katie's sweater and removed her bra. She used to be self-conscious about her body, especially during pregnancy. But now, thanks to Joe's healing powers, when she looked in the mirror, she saw the body she had back in college, maybe even better. That pleased her.

Chapter 3

The next morning, Joe made breakfast while Katie got ready. He timed it just right, putting the food on the table a minute after Katie carried her coffee into the dining room and sat down. Joe had cooked bacon and eggs again. He sat down next to Katie, who took a bite of her eggs and said, "Thanks for making breakfast this morning, Honey."

"I told you before, you don't need to thank me. We both contribute to this marriage, and cooking is my contribution."

"Well, you contribute more than I do, and I want you to know I appreciate it."

"That's not true. You handle all the mundane tasks, like paying bills. You drive us everywhere. You help me remember things. Your marketing keeps the resort full. Oh, and you got us a big discount from that chimney sweep guy last month."

"I had nothing to do with that. He was just being nice."

"I'm pretty sure if I were here alone, he would not have been as nice."

"Maybe not, but whenever we go to Gretchen's, we always get great service because of you. I think Patty is attracted to you."

"Patty? Seriously? Don't tell me you're jealous. She must be over fifty."

Katie took a bite of her bacon. After swallowing, she said, "You're over a hundred. What's your point?"

"You know what I mean."

"Are you saying I should only be worried about women under thirty?"

"No! I didn't say that. You're twisting my words."

Katie smiled. "Relax. I'm not jealous. I think it's cute."

"Cute? Do you mean cute like when old man Murphy cuts my hair and is distracted the entire time because you are sitting there waiting for me?"

Katie put her hand on Joe's leg, smiled, and said, "He must know I'm attracted to centenarians."

"Oh, you're a load of laughs," Joe said as he tickled Katie.

She laughed and held up her hand. "Wait! Stop! We can mess around later. We need to get ready so we can help Jenna and Mitch."

"Of course, my dear. Finish your breakfast and stop delaying us."

Thirty minutes later, when they were on the road, Katie called her parents. The call went through her car's speakers so Joe could hear it, too. Mary answered and said, "Good morning, Honey. Did you sleep well last night without Joey to keep you up?"

Katie looked at Joe. They both smiled. "Uh, yeah. Sure. Joey usually doesn't keep us up anymore. Was he okay with you?"

"Oh, he was terrible. He kept crying and saying 'Mama.'"

Katie thought for a few seconds and said, "You're just saying that to make me feel better."

"I never could fool you, Honey. Actually, he's a great kid. I wish you were this well-behaved when you were a year old."

"Give him time. He hasn't learned what he can get away with from you yet."

"Don't worry. We can handle him."

"Okay, Mom. Thanks so much for taking care of Joey for us. I don't know what we would do without you and Dad."

"You would manage fine. Concentrate on helping Jenna and Mitch, and don't worry about a thing."

When the call ended, Katie's smile faded. She stared at the road ahead for a long moment. She couldn't shake the feeling that the stakes were too high and they might not be up to the task. She turned to Joe and asked, "What if we fail? What if we can't prove Mitch is innocent, and he goes to prison? I don't know if I could live with myself if that happened."

"That is a possibility, but it wouldn't be your fault. We've had some good successes in the past, but we aren't perfect."

"That's what worries me. We never had a person depending on us for their freedom like we do now."

"What about Daniel Erickson?"

"The senator? His freedom was a byproduct of our investigation, not the catalyst. It's different now. Whatever we do or don't do will have a direct effect on my best childhood friend and her husband. If we fail, her family will be torn apart."

"Have you considered the possibility that Mitch is guilty? I mean, even good people sometimes do bad things. Maybe it was an accident."

Katie looked at Joe. "No! I know Mitch. He's no killer. You could show me a video of him committing the crime, and I would tell you it's a deep fake."

"What's a deep fake?"

Katie shook her head. "It doesn't matter."

"Alright, Katie. We'll start with the assumption that the cops are wrong."

Katie put her hand on Joe's and said, "We should let Jenna know we're on the way." She dialed her number and told her they would be there in less than three hours. Jenna said she was home and would wait for them.

***

They arrived in Katie's hometown almost two and a half hours later. The town lay on the Mississippi River, near the same latitude as the resort. To get there, they had to follow the highway as it meandered south, then take another road heading north.

As they drove into town, they passed a decorative wooden sign with carved lettering that read, "Welcome to Minaka." The sign was dark green with white lettering. Below the sign hung a smaller sign with the words "Population 3400."

Two blocks before reaching the downtown area, Katie pulled into the driveway of her parents' house. To Katie, it felt like a bittersweet homecoming. The split-level home featured a single-story section to the right, while the left side rose to two stories, including a half-basement. A two-car garage jutted forward from the left end.

Directly across the street was a parking lot for a V.F.W. post. When the parking lot was empty, there was a clear view of the Mississippi River, which was a little over a block away.

"Are you happy to be home?" Joe asked as Katie put the car in park.

"My home is with you now."

"I mean, are you happy to be back where you grew up?"

"I am, but I wish it were under happier circumstances."

Joe nodded but said nothing before they got out of the car. The air was cold, but not freezing. The faint smell of burning wood entered Joe's nose, probably from a nearby fireplace. He looked around and said, "It must have been nice growing up with such a beautiful view."

"I guess. I don't think I paid attention to it when I was young. Being a photographer, you have a better eye for beauty than I do."

"Everyone can enjoy beauty," Joe said as he pulled their suitcase out of the car.

"Yeah, but you see beauty in things that I miss."

"You only miss it because you are busy thinking about other things."

Katie unlocked the door, and they went inside. The living room was to the right. Polished hardwood floors gleamed with light from the large window. A leather sofa sat against the wall opposite the window. A fireplace dominated the far wall. On either side of it, two chairs sat like stone lions guarding the entrance to a bridge. The room had no television and was primarily used for entertaining guests.

To their left were stairs that led up to the bedrooms, and beyond them were more stairs leading down to the family room. They went upstairs to Katie's bedroom, where Joe set the suitcase on the bed.

"Just so you know," Katie said, "I'm busy thinking about other things because I have other things more important to think about."

Joe nodded. "That you do, my dear."

Katie put her arms around Joe and hugged him. "Thank you for doing this with me and not giving me a hard time."

"A hard time? Me? When have I ever given you a hard time?"

"Well, last year, when I wanted to help investigate the killing of Steven North, you didn't want to. You thought I was too pregnant. Before that, there was the killing at the resort that you thought the police should handle. Oh, and before that..."

"Okay! Okay! I get it. Those times I was worried about you and the baby. Now, I'm not worried as much. Plus, a man's life is at stake."

"Yeah. Speaking of that, we need to go see Jenna. I'm sure she's learned something by now."

Katie and Joe drove to Jenna's house, which was three blocks east of Katie's parents' home. All the snow had melted after a few days of above-freezing temperatures, leaving the yards they passed covered in brown grass and mud. They turned onto Jenna's street, where maple trees lined both sides, their bare branches silhouetted against the gray morning sky.

The house was a one-story Craftsman nestled between two similar houses. A deep porch stretched across the entire front of the house, its roof supported by four tapered columns resting on brick bases. The vinyl siding was a soft green surrounded by white trim. A brick chimney extended above the steeply sloped roof on the left side of the house. The flower boxes beneath the windows probably added a colorful touch to the home during the warmer months, but they now contained only dirt.

Katie turned into the driveway and eased to a stop behind a blue Toyota Rav4, which looked overdue for a car wash. They got out of the car and stepped onto the damp concrete as a blue jay flew past them and landed on a tree in the front yard. They both watched the bird briefly and then climbed the two steps onto the porch. Katie rang the doorbell, and they waited.

A few moments later, Jenna opened the door and smiled when she saw Katie. It was a tired smile, but it still lit up her face. Strands of copper-red hair blew in front of her blue eyes as she opened her arms and hugged Katie. She then hugged Joe and said, "Thank you both for coming."

"You don't have to thank us," Katie said. "That's what friends do."

Jenna opened the door wide and said, "Come on inside."

Katie stepped through the door, followed by Joe. Once inside, they both removed their shoes.

"You don't have to do that," Jenna said.

"It's a habit. We do it at our house," Katie said before looking at Joe and adding, "Usually."

The home was old but clean and modern-looking on the inside. It appeared they had recently updated it. The bedrooms were to the right. To the left was the living room, where a fireplace stood against the far wall. A large television hung on the wall to its left. A sofa and two chairs made a half circle around the television and fireplace. The living room transitioned seamlessly into the kitchen at the back of the house.

Jenna led Katie and Joe to the living room and invited them to sit on the sofa while she sat in the chair next to them. Joe had been to Katie's hometown a few times over the last couple of years. Each visit, they spent time with Jenna and Mitch, but Joe had never been inside their house before. "Your home is lovely," he said. "Do you use the fireplace?"

"Mitch will usually light a fire in the evenings. We enjoy sitting by it after the kids go to bed. At least we used to." Jenna said before she started crying.

Katie leaned over and put her hand on Jenna's. "Don't worry. We'll figure it out. Have you learned anything new since we last spoke?"

"I was finally able to talk to Mitch late yesterday afternoon," she said. "He told me he was driving home from work. The parking lot for his office sits on 3rd Street, which runs behind the police station. He said he saw a body lying on the ground behind the station when he drove by, so naturally, he stopped the car to check to see if the person was okay. He said the body was facedown and didn't know who he was until he rolled him over. That's when the chief appeared. Mitch tried to explain what happened, but the chief was sure he had murdered David and wouldn't listen."

Katie shook her head in disbelief. "What terrible timing. How was David killed?"

"Someone hit him on the head with a tire iron. They think Mitch slashed David's tire and then killed him when he attempted to change it."

"Surely finding him at the scene can't be enough to charge him with the crime, much less convict him," Joe said.

"Mitch and David have a history," Jenna said. "In high school, David was what you would call a jock. He was captain of the football team and could always get pretty much any girl he wanted."

"Including you," Katie added.

"Yes," Jenna said. "We dated for a little while. He was a senior and I was a junior. I'm embarrassed to admit I was taken in by his charm."

"How does this relate to Mitch?" Joe asked.

"Mitch was a bit of a nerd in high school and tended to get picked on by some of the jocks, especially David, who was a year older and much bigger than him at the time."

"I never got the impression that Mitch was a skinny little nerd," Joe said.

"He's changed a lot since high school. He started working out in college and gained a confidence he didn't have previously. We ran into each other at Christmastime one year, when we were both home from college. I didn't recognize him at first, but before long, we were dating. The rest is history."

"Getting picked on in high school is not a motive for murder more than a decade later," Katie said.

Jenna hesitated, then added, "There's more. David got divorced last summer. Since then, he's been hitting on me. He wanted me to break up with Mitch and get back together with him. In his mind, he was such a great catch and couldn't understand why I would pick Mitch over him."

"I can see why that would anger Mitch," Joe said.

"It started innocently enough. David came to the hospital while I was working to interview a crime victim. We said hello and talked for a little while, and then he left. Over the next couple of months, he would visit the hospital more frequently. His attempts to sway me grew increasingly bold. I finally decided to tell Mitch, and he was pissed."

"What happened then?" Katie asked.

"Mitch took the day off from work and spent the entire morning at the hospital. David showed up and, in front of several people, Mitch told him that if he didn't stop harassing me, he'd kill him. I know it was stupid for him to say that, but he didn't mean it literally. He's not that kind of guy. The worst thing is, I was happy he told him off. I felt so proud of him that day. Now I wish I had never told him what was going on." She started crying again.

Katie touched her hand again. "It's not your fault. He needed to know. A man's job is to protect their woman. It's written in their DNA. If you didn't tell him, he would have found out another way, and then he would have been angry at both you and David."

Jenna wiped her eyes with a tissue. "I suppose you're right."

"When did that happen?" Joe asked.

"A little over a week ago."

"What did Mitch's lawyer say?" Joe asked.

"She said it could go either way. She suggested he plead guilty to second-degree murder to avoid a life sentence."

"That's ridiculous," Katie said. "Who's his lawyer? I think he needs a new one."

"His lawyer is Emily Anderson."

"Emily? Really? Isn't she a bit young? What happened to Eddie Langston?"

"He retired last year, and Emily is the only criminal attorney left in town. Besides, we can't afford a big city lawyer."

"Can't a lawyer at Mitch's firm help him?" Joe asked.

"They practice family law. If he wanted a will or a divorce, sure, but not for murder. Don't worry about Emily. She's a smart girl."

"I know, but does she have the experience?" Katie asked.

"She's three years younger than us. You're still thinking of her as that fourteen-year-old girl you knew, but we've all grown older. I mean, you still look like you're twenty-two, but a lot of years have passed since you dated her brother."

"Brother?" Joe said, surprised. "Is he the one who cheated on you?"

"You told him about Jimmy?" Jenna asked.

"Yeah. The subject came up last year. I wanted to forget about that part of my life."

"If it makes you feel any better, Jimmy's been divorced twice already."

"Do you think I would be so shallow that I would wish bad things on Jimmy?"

"I would," Jenna said.

"I hate to admit it, but I am a little glad. Hopefully, he got a taste of his own medicine."

"Can we talk to Mitch?" Joe asked, attempting to change the subject.

"Yes, of course. I'll call the jail and ask them to put you and Katie on the visitor list."

"Aren't you coming with us?" Katie asked.

"I want to, but I can't. Sophia is sick."

"Oh, no," Katie said. "What's wrong with her?"

"She woke up this morning with a sore throat and a mild fever."

"What about Lucas?" Katie asked.

"He seemed fine. My parents are watching him. I didn't want him to catch whatever Sophia has."

"I thought it seemed quiet around here. If you want, Joe can help Sophia feel better."

Jenna looked at Joe. "That's right. Katie told me you were quite knowledgeable about health. Do you think you can help her?"

"I can certainly try," Joe said.

"He's being modest," Katie said. "He can definitely help her."

"Okay then. Follow me."

She led them down the hallway and opened her daughter's bedroom door. Sophia was eight years old. Her hair had a hint of red, like her mom's, but it was closer to brown and straighter than her mom's hair. She lay in bed, propped up against two pillows with the covers pulled up. She watched a cartoon playing on a television that sat on the dresser at the foot of the bed. "How are you feeling, Honey?" Jenna asked.

"My throat still hurts. I think it feels worse."

"Do you remember my friends, Katie and Joe?"

Sophia looked at them and nodded.

"Joe is going to look at you to see if he can help you feel better. Is that okay?"

Sophia nodded again.

Joe moved next to her and held her right hand with his right hand while putting his left hand on her forehead. He didn't need to feel her forehead, but he wanted Jenna to think he was feeling her temperature. Instead, he connected to her. He could feel her body's immune system struggling with an invader. After a few seconds, he knew what it was. "She has a bacterial infection. Her body is fighting it off, but it needs help."

"How do you know that?" Jenna asked.

"Katie touched her arm. "It's best not to ask how. Just trust that he knows what he's doing. I promise Sophia will be fine by this evening."

Joe removed his hand from Sophia's forehead and used both of his hands to press on her hand. "We need to encourage her body to produce more antibodies to fight the infection. There are certain pressure points on our hands that, if manipulated just right, can help with that."

33

Joe had learned that pretending to be a reflexologist was a good way to avoid questions about how he was able to cure others. Nobody understood reflexology, including Joe. People just assumed he knew what he was doing and didn't care about a lengthy explanation of how the body worked.

Joe instructed Sophia's body to produce as many antibodies as physically possible. After a few minutes, he let go of her hand and said, "She'll be fine. She needs rest. Rest is a time of healing. It will take a few hours for her immune system to get ahead of the infection. You can give her a little honey to soothe her throat. If she's not better by dinnertime, let me know."

"Dinnertime? That soon? Are you sure?"

"He's sure," Katie said. "Joe is a miracle worker."

"Maybe we should go see Mitch now," Joe said, attempting again to change the subject.

"Yes, of course," Jenna said as they walked out of Sophia's bedroom. "Please tell him why I couldn't come with you and tell him I love him."

Chapter 4

Katie and Joe drove to the county jail, which was more than thirty miles from Minaka. The building was a large, two-story brick structure with the county courthouse on the right side and the jail on the left. Katie parked the car on the jail side, and they entered through a door labeled "Visitor Check-in."

After going through a security checkpoint, a uniformed deputy, behind glass, greeted them and asked, "Who are you here to see?"

"Mitchell Hartney," Katie said.

"What are your names?"

"Katie and Joe Novak," Katie said.

The deputy picked up a clipboard and flipped through multiple pieces of paper. When he found the right one, he removed it and slid it under the opening. "Sign this and print your names, please. I will also need to see your identification."

Katie and Joe both signed the paper and returned it through the slot. After they both pressed their driver's licenses against the glass, the deputy pushed a button, causing the door to buzz. "Go ahead through," he said.

They met another deputy on the other side of the door, who made them wait for several minutes before ushering them into a small, dimly lit room. There were five booths in the room, each with a thick, glass window. The booths were separated by small partitions that offered little privacy. Stools bolted to the floor stood in front of each window. A telephone hung on the right divider in each booth. Nobody else was in the room.

The deputy directed Katie and Joe to the booth on the right. Katie sat on the stool, and Joe stood behind her and to her right. Mitch sat on the stool opposite Katie.

Joe had seen Mitch a few times before, and he was always well-groomed and upbeat. Now he looked like a different person. His face looked tired. His light brown hair was a mess, and he needed a shave. He wore an orange, V-neck, short-sleeve shirt and orange pants. Joe had seen one-piece prison jumpsuits before and thought Mitch was lucky he wasn't issued one of those. He assumed going to the bathroom was a huge pain for those prisoners.

Mitch picked up his telephone at the same time Katie picked up hers. "Hello, Katie. Hello, Joe. It's good to see you again, although I wish it were under better circumstances."

Katie turned the phone away from her ear so Joe could hear better. "We do, too," she said. "How are you doing in there?"

"I'm as well as can be expected. How are Jenna and the kids?"

"Jenna is worried, as you'd expect. Sophia was sick today. That's why she couldn't be here."

"Oh, no. What's wrong with Sophia?

"A bit of a sore throat, but don't worry. It's not serious. She'll be fine by this afternoon."

"I hope you're right."

Joe, attempting to speed things up, leaned toward the phone and said, "We only have a short time, so we should talk about your case."

"Did Jenna ask you to look into what happened?" Mitch asked.

Katie looked at Joe and then back at Mitch. "We volunteered."

"I want you guys to know right up front that I really appreciate what you are doing for me. Even if you fail, I will always be grateful. I heard the cops have given up looking for another suspect. They're certain I'm guilty. You're my last hope."

"We need to know exactly what happened," Joe said.

"Well, our law office is just down the road from the police station. I left work a little early, which I usually do on Friday, and headed home. My route takes me past the back of the police station. That's where the squad cars and employee vehicles are parked. As I passed by, I noticed what appeared to be a body lying on the ground. I stopped to check it out. I didn't know who it was, but when I got close, I saw blood on the back of his head and knew it was bad. I gently turned him over and saw it was David. I removed my gloves and checked for a pulse, but couldn't find one. That's when I stood up to look for a police officer to whom I could yell. One saw me first. It was the chief."

"So, the chief arrested you?" Katie asked.

"Yes, technically. When he saw who was on the ground, he was not nice to say the least. He held me at gunpoint and called for backup. Before I knew it, every officer in the building was manhandling me. I tried to explain I didn't do it, but no one would listen."

"When you say 'manhandling,' do you mean they beat you?" Joe asked.

"No. I wouldn't say that, but they were overly aggressive when they shoved me against the car and handcuffed me."

"Did you see anyone else in the parking lot besides the chief?" Katie asked.

"No. Whoever did it was long gone by the time I arrived."

"We need to ask you about the incident at the hospital," Katie said.

"Oh, yeah. Not my brightest moment. David was harassing Jenna, and I couldn't let that continue. In the past, he was always the one intimidating me. I figured I would try to intimidate him for a change. I thought if I acted crazy, he might believe I was crazy and back off. That plan backfired. Instead of threatening him, I should have just punched him in the face."

"If you had, you might still be in the same boat," Katie said. "What did Dave say after you threatened to kill him?"

"That's the weird part. He laughed and said, 'I didn't know you had it in you, Mitch.' Then the hospital security intervened and separated us. I never saw him after that, and neither did Jenna, so maybe it worked."

"If he stopped bothering Jenna, that would take away your motive for murder," Joe said.

"Yeah, right. Tell the cops that. I'm sure they will all get a good laugh. They found me next to a dead body a week after I threatened to kill him. What kind of dumb luck is that?"

"What did your lawyer say about it?" Katie asked.

"She said it could go either way. She said she might be able to work a deal and get the charge dropped to second-degree murder if I plead guilty. Then I would be eligible for parole after 20 years."

"That's still harsh," Katie said.

"It's especially harsh for an innocent man. I'm not going to plead guilty to something I didn't do. I'll roll the dice and take a chance."

"We will do everything in our power to prove you are innocent," Katie said.

"I know you will, and I really appreciate it."

***

On the way back to town, Katie said, "I think we should talk to the police. Jenna's sister is a cop now. Maybe she can tell us something useful."

Joe nodded. "I thought she was in the Army."

"That's old news."

"Okay, but let's stop for lunch first. I'm starving."

"There's a place near here that serves Lebanese food. It's not fancy, but the food is good."

"Lebanese food sounds good to me. When Marie and I lived in New York, our Lebanese neighbors made the best Tabbouleh. I tried to duplicate it, but never could get it to taste as good."

"That's surprising considering you are so good in the kitchen."

"No matter how good one gets, there is always someone better."

"Not necessarily. Somebody has to be the best. I can't imagine any healers out there better than you."

"Maybe in some ways I'm the best, but I can only direct a person's body to heal itself. I can't make a finger grow back, but a surgeon can sew it back on and make it work. If you were to lose a finger, I would bring you straight to the hospital."

"Are you sure you can't make a finger grow back? Have you ever tried?"

"Well, no, but humans aren't like lizards. We can't grow limbs back."

"Humans can't consciously tell their bodies how to heal, but you can. Maybe you can instruct someone's body how to regrow itself."

"I hope I never have to. Even if I could, it would take way too long. I would need to be connected to that person for weeks while the body part grew back."

"I guess that would be unrealistic, but it might work on you."

"Again, I hope I never have to find out."

After stopping for lunch, they headed to the police station. The two-story brick structure stood near the center of town. Katie parked in one of the designated spaces in front of the building. They walked up the four concrete steps, and Joe pulled one of the large wooden doors open, holding it for Katie before following her inside.

The room was small. It reminded Joe of the pediatrician's office where he took his kids when they were young. Six uncomfortable-looking chairs, three against each wall, sat on the hard tile floor. A young officer sat behind a desk. Behind him, to his right, were two closed doors, both with frosted glass windows. To his left was an arched opening leading to another room, mostly obscured from view. They approached the officer, and Katie said, "Hi. We want to talk to Officer Cheryl Ripley."

"Officer Ripley is out on patrol. Can I ask what your business is with her?"

"It's a personal matter. Do you know when she'll be back?"

"What are your names?" the officer asked.

"Katie and Joe Novak," Katie said.

"Just a minute." The officer picked up his radio mic and pushed the button. "Unit three, Officer Ripley. Copy?"

Cheryl's voice crackled over the radio. "Go ahead."

"Be advised, there is a Katie and Joe Novak here to see you."

After a short pause, Cheryl said, "Copy that. I'll be there in five minutes."

When the officer hung up the mic, Katie said, "Thanks so much."

They sat and waited. Joe flipped through the magazine rack next to his chair but found nothing interesting. Most were gossip-type magazines, and all were more than five years old. He assumed they had canceled the magazine subscriptions because people were too busy looking at their phones to read them.

True to her word, Cheryl arrived five minutes later. She came through the archway behind the officer at the desk, still wearing her winter coat. She walked around to the lobby and hugged Katie. "It's good to see you again," she said. She then hugged Joe and said, "Let's talk outside."

They walked out the main door and down the steps, stopping on the sidewalk. "Jenna said you came to help Mitch."

"That's right," Katie said.

"You need to watch your step. Mitch is public enemy number one around here."

"Do you think he's guilty?" Joe asked.

"I'll be honest, I don't know what to believe. I don't think it's in Mitch's character to commit murder, but he did threaten to kill David and then was caught standing over the body."

"If Mitch wanted to kill David, don't you think he would have found a better place to do it than at the police station?" Katie asked.

"Maybe they got into a big argument, and it just happened in the heat of passion," Cheryl said. "As a cop, I have seen many instances where a domestic squabble turned violent."

"Are you siding with everyone else here?" Katie asked.

"No, Katie. I want to know the truth as much as you do. I'm just saying that you can't discount the possibility that Mitch might be guilty."

"I can discount it," Katie said. "I'm certain he is innocent."

"Are you investigating other possibilities?" Joe asked.

"Not as far as I know. It doesn't help that our only detective is dead. Sergeant Daniels is leading the investigation, but he is stretched thin with all his own work plus David's work."

"That's why you need us here," Katie said.

"I agree," Cheryl said, "but don't expect much help from Chief Bronson."

"I hope we can at least count on your help," Katie said.

"Of course. I'll do whatever I can."

"Is there anything you can tell us about what happened that day?" Katie asked.

"No. I was out on patrol when everything went down. I doubt I know any more than you do." Cheryl reached into her pocket and took out a business card. "This has my cell phone number. If there's anything I can do to help, call me."

"Thanks so much, Cheryl," Katie said.

Cheryl went back inside the police station while Katie and Joe headed back to the car. Once inside, Joe asked, "Can we drive around the back of the police station? I want to see what Mitch saw that day."

"Of course," Katie said before pulling out and doing a U-turn. She turned left onto the first street. The building on the left housed an accountant and a barber shop. Next to the barber shop was a street, and beyond the street was Mitch's law firm. Katie turned left onto the street.

On the right, behind the building, was the law firm's parking lot. There was another parking area behind the barber shop on the left. Beyond the barber shop's parking area was the police station's parking lot. There was a grassy area, now mostly dirt, between the two parking lots.

Katie drove slowly past the police lot. There was one police car and four civilian cars parked in the small lot, including David's car, an older-model, blue Ford Mustang with a flat tire. Orange traffic cones with crime scene tape wrapped around them surrounded the car.

"Stop here," Joe said.

Katie pulled over, and they both got out of the car. They walked to within a few feet of David's car and stopped. They both looked around.

"There are no barriers between parking lots," Katie said. "Someone could have easily entered and left the lot quickly."

Joe scanned all of the nearby buildings but didn't see what he was looking for. "There are also no cameras that I can see."

"This isn't going to be easy," Katie said. "There are no people around. The odds that we'll find a witness are slim to none."

"I agree. I think we should talk to Mitch's lawyer."

"It's Sunday. We'll have to wait until tomorrow morning."

"So, what do you think we should do the rest of the day?" Joe asked.

Katie looked at Joe, smiled, and said, "We are alone without a child to look after. What do you think we should do?"

Joe paused briefly and said, "I can't help but think this is a trick question. What is it that you want to do?"

"Let's pick up a pizza, go back to my parents' house, and watch a movie."

"I suspected it was a trick question," Joe said.

Katie laughed, put a hand on Joe's arm, and said, "Don't worry, Honey. We can do that, too."

Chapter 5

Katie and Joe were awakened the next morning by a rooster crowing. Joe looked out the window and said, "It's still dark outside. Who keeps roosters in the middle of a town?"

"That must be Jack Nash," Katie said. "Dad has complained about him a few times. He said he's raising chickens for eggs."

"You don't need a rooster for that."

"That's what I said, but Jack thinks a rooster keeps the chickens in line so they lay more eggs."

Joe found the switch on his lamp and turned it on. "That must be because women need men in their lives."

Katie rolled her eyes. "Really? The reality is, men need women more than women need men."

"Untrue. If you put a hundred men on one deserted island and a hundred women on another, after two months, the men would be thriving while the women would be starving."

I don't know about that. What I do know is the men would have split up into warring factions while the women would remain united as one."

"Not if some of the women were ovulating," Joe said.

"Are we really going to start the day arguing?"

"You're right, Katie. Let's agree that men and women need each other."

"Okay, I agree. I need you to make me coffee."

They both got up and showered together. Before long, they were in the throes of passion.

Afterward, Joe made coffee for Katie while she got ready. He preferred orange juice in the morning, but he couldn't find any in the refrigerator. He did find a container of apple juice and poured himself a glass while the coffee was brewing. He then looked through the fridge for eggs and bacon, but found neither. He checked the cabinet, but the only breakfast food he could see was a box of corn flakes.

When the coffee was ready, he carried a cup up to Katie's bedroom. "There's nothing to eat for breakfast," he said. "We'll have to go out this morning."

"That's fine with me," Katie said. "There's a good breakfast restaurant downtown."

"That's great," Joe said. "I think we should walk there."

"You want to walk? It's thirty degrees outside."

"Are you saying you can't handle thirty degrees?"

"Of course I can. Okay, fine. Let's walk there."

When they were ready, they put on their coats and walked toward the restaurant. They held hands on the way. "Doesn't it feel good to get out into the fresh air?" Joe asked.

"Yeah. Much better than driving in a warm car."

Joe stopped walking but kept hold of Katie's hand, which made her stop as well. "If you want to drive, that's fine with me. We can go back and get the car."

"No, no. It's fine. I'm sure walking is good for us." They continued walking. After a few steps, she added, "Even though we are both in perfect health."

This time, Joe ignored the comment and continued walking. When she was pregnant, he felt like he had to cater to her every whim, but now he thought a walk would be good for her mental health, which was not something he could fix with his healing abilities.

It took them about five minutes to walk to the restaurant. It was less than a block from the police station on the same side of the road. Joe opened the door for Katie and followed her inside. A friendly, middle-aged woman greeted them with a smile, picked up a couple of menus, and led them to the only available table near the back of the restaurant. "Your server will be with you shortly," she said before walking away.

The server showed up a short time later and took their drink order. While they waited, Katie took out her phone and said, "I want to see how Joey's doing," before dialing her mom.

"I'm sure he's fine," Joe said.

Her mom answered, and Katie put the phone on speaker so Joe could hear.

"Hi, Mom. Joe and I were just wondering how you and Dad are getting along with Joey?"

"We're doing great, Honey. Joey's a good kid. You have nothing to worry about."

"I know, but I can't help it."

"I understand. I wish I could say it gets easier, but I still worry about you after all these years."

"You don't have to worry about me, Mom."

"Really? You were almost killed in an explosion and then kidnapped twice. Let's not even talk about that crazy woman who had you at gunpoint or the crooked cop who tried to arrest you."

"Okay, I see your point, but how do you even know any of those? Other than the explosion, I never mentioned any of those things to you."

"I'm your mother, Honey. Do you think I don't follow your news stories?"

"I didn't think you could watch Milwaukee news stations out here."

"We have something called the internet now. Have you heard of it?"

Joe laughed. Katie often teased him about his limited knowledge of technology. Now she was getting a taste of her own medicine. "It looks like the shoe is on the other foot," he said.

Katie turned to Joe with an annoyed look on her face. "We don't need to hear anything from the peanut gallery," she said. She then turned her attention to her mom. "Can we say hi to Joey?"

"Sorry, but he's not here. It snowed here last night, and your father took him outside to build a snowman."

"A snowman? He's a year old. He can't build a snowman."

"Maybe not, but your father can. Don't worry. I'm sure they'll both have fun. I don't know about Joey, but Dad could sure benefit from a bit of playtime."

The server arrived with their drinks, and Katie said, "I have to go, Mom. I'll call you later."

After they ordered their food, Katie added cream to her coffee while Joe sipped his orange juice. He set the glass down and asked, "How long are you willing to commit to this investigation? I mean, your parents have to go back to work next week."

"Do you think it will take longer than a week?"

"I don't know. Some investigations go on for years."

"I suppose if we haven't learned anything by the weekend, we will either have to give up or bring Joey here."

"I think that is a good incentive to work hard," Joe said.

"Mitch rotting in jail is incentive enough."

"Good point."

***

After breakfast, they walked to Emily Anderson's law firm. It occupied part of the ground floor of an old, three-story brick building situated on a prime corner where the two main roads in town intersected. The top two floors were apartments, while the bottom floor was commercial.

The law office was next to a furniture store that occupied the two units closest to the corner. All the businesses in the building had dark red awnings with their names in white lettering. The awning over the law office said, "Langston & Anderson, P.A." Joe opened the door and held it for Katie before following her inside.

The reception area was small, but welcoming. A table with a lamp stood between two wooden chairs with leather cushions. The lamp and several overhead fixtures emitted a soft, warm light. The walls were painted beige, with a chestnut-colored wainscoting along the bottom. A young woman sat behind an oak desk, a pile of manila folders at her side. To her left, a view of the downtown area was visible through a large window.

The woman looked up and said, "Hello. How can I help you?"

"We need to speak with Emily Anderson," Katie said.

"Do you have an appointment?"

"No. It's about the Mitchell Hartney case," Katie said.

"Who should I say is asking?"

"Katie and Joe Novak."

"Just a minute," the woman said before disappearing down the hallway.

When she returned, she said, "Ms. Anderson will see you now." She then led them to her office before returning to work.

Emily Anderson sat behind a large L-shaped desk as Katie and Joe entered her office. A computer screen sat on the far-left side of the desk. File folders occupied most of the remaining space. She had one folder open in front of her, reading its contents. Without looking up, she said, "Have a seat. I'll be with you in a moment."

Katie and Joe sat in the two chairs in front of the desk. After several seconds, Emily Anderson looked up and said, "What can I do for you?" As soon as those words came out of her mouth, a flash of recognition crossed her face. "Katie? Katie Kowalczyk? Is that you?"

Without waiting for a response, she excitedly got up from her chair. Katie stood up, too, and the two women hugged. "I don't believe it," Emily said. "I haven't seen you since high school. You look great. I heard you became some big-time investigative reporter in Milwaukee."

"I don't know about big-time. Anyway, I don't do that anymore, except occasionally as a freelance reporter."

"Really? What happened with that job?"

"Well, I got married a couple of years ago and moved away from Milwaukee. This is my husband, Joe."

Joe shook Emily's hand. "It's nice to meet you, Emily."

Everyone sat back down, and Emily asked, "So, what do you do now?"

"Joe owns a ski resort a couple of hours east of here. I'm the marketing director."

She looked at Joe and said, "Wow! That's impressive for someone as young as you." She turned her attention back to Katie. "Why are you here? Lynn, my assistant, said it was about the Hartney case."

"We came here to prove Mitch Hartney is innocent," Katie said.

Emily tilted her head. "Really? Why are you interested in this case?"

"Because I know Mitch. I know he's a good man who would never murder anyone. Also, because he's married to Jenna, and I want to help them."

"Oh, that's right. You and Jenna were best friends, if I remember right."

"You remember right. I've known those two for years, and I'm certain Mitch is innocent."

"Unfortunately, unless I get Mitch's written permission, I can't share details about his case with you."

"When will you see him again?"

Emily looked at her watch. "I need to leave soon. Mitch is scheduled to come before the judge at eleven. I'll get his permission when I see him, and then we can talk about the case. Do you think you can learn something that the police can't?"

"We hope so," Katie said. "Jenna doesn't believe the police will do anything to look for other possible suspects."

"I hate to say it, but she is probably right. If I'm going to defend Mitch properly, I'll need evidence that supports his side of the story, and I doubt I will get it from the police. I'll need some additional help."

"What are you saying, exactly?" Katie asked.

"I'm saying, why don't you two work for me? There's no money in the budget, so you'll have to work pro bono, but if you're willing, it would be a big help."

"We are already investigating the case," Joe said. "Why should we work for you?"

"Because you would be officially gathering evidence for Mitchell Hartney's attorney. That means that if any member of the police department tries to hinder your investigation, they would be guilty of interfering with my client's right to a fair trial. I'm sure they won't want to risk a mistrial."

Katie looked at Joe, who nodded. She looked back at Emily and said, "If we solve this case, would I be allowed to report it on the news?"

"Of course," Emily said. "You won't be able to reveal any private communications, but you are free to report anything else."

"One last question," Katie said. "Are you aware we are not licensed private investigators?"

"That's not a problem. Wisconsin has no requirements for you to be licensed."

"Okay, then. It seems you now have investigators on your team."

"That's great. I look forward to working with you both. We'll discuss Mitch's case after I see him and get his okay."

When they left the law office, Katie felt empowered, as if she had been promoted. "Let's go to the police station and talk to the chief."

"I doubt he will cooperate in helping us prove Mitch's innocence," Joe said.

"We're working for the defense team now. He won't be able to dismiss us legally."

"Okay, we'll see how that goes."

***

They walked to the police station and found Cheryl behind the reception desk. Katie was pleased to see her there. "Good morning, Cheryl. I see you have desk duty today."

"Hi, guys. Yeah, we all take a turn, but it's not all day. What brings you back?"

"We want to talk to the chief," Katie said.

Cheryl looked toward the chief's office, then back at Katie. "Are you sure? He's not in the best of moods today."

"I don't think there will be a better time," Katie said.

"He's in there with his son right now. It may be a few minutes."

"That's fine," Katie said before she and Joe sat down to wait.

After five minutes, the chief's door opened, and they saw the chief standing inside the doorway. He hugged his son, who looked a lot like him, except his hair was much darker and he was a few inches shorter. Even so, he was at least as tall as Joe, maybe taller. The son stepped out of the office and walked past Katie and Joe while the chief closed his door.

When the son walked outside, Cheryl said softly, "He comes in a lot since his mom died."

Katie stood up and stepped closer to Cheryl. Joe rose and stood next to Katie. "I didn't realize the chief's wife had died," Katie said. "When did it happen? What did she die of?"

"She passed away early last summer from cancer. It was a real shame. She was only forty-five."

"That's terrible," Katie said. "I wish we had known sooner."

"It's not like there would have been anything you could have done about it."

Katie looked at Joe and back at Cheryl. "No. I guess not."

"Anyway, she died before I started this job, but I hear the chief and his son are closer now than ever. Personally, I think his son takes advantage of him."

"Oh, yeah? In what way?" Katie asked.

"Well, he's twenty-three years old, has a good job at the mill, and still borrows money from his dad like he's a teenager. The chief can't say no to him."

"What does he do for a living?" Katie asked.

"He's an electrical engineer or something like that. He's been working at the mill since he graduated from college. I'm sure he makes a good living, but it seems he always needs money for something, and the chief gives in every time."

"Does he have a drug or gambling problem?" Joe asked.

"I don't think so. I heard he wastes his money on frivolous things, then can't pay his rent. I think the chief feels bad for him, even though he's a grown man."

"I can understand that," Joe said. "If Katie died, I would feel like I needed to give Joey twice the attention."

Katie looked at Joe and shook her head. "Joey's a year old. We're talking about a grown adult here."

"I know, but even so, I would probably want to overcompensate for your loss."

"You have a good heart, Joe, but sometimes giving your child too much attention can be a bad thing," Katie said.

"Look at you being the wise one. I know you're right, but it can be difficult to think logically in emotional situations."

"Yeah, I guess so. I would probably feel the same way if you died before me."

Cheryl shook her head and spoke at a normal volume. "Let's stop talking about dying. I'll check if the chief will see you now."

She got up and walked to the chief's office, which was the closest door behind the reception desk. She knocked and went inside. When she returned thirty seconds later, she said, "Go ahead in, and good luck."

Katie pushed open the door and went inside, followed by Joe, who closed the door behind him. "Good morning, Chief Bronson," Katie said.

The chief stood, smiled, and said, "Katie Kowalczyk. It's good to see you again."

"It's Novak now. This is my husband, Joe."

They exchanged greetings, and the chief invited them to sit down.

"We just heard about your wife," Katie said. "We're so sorry."

"Thank you," he said. "So, how's the news business going? Are you here to do a story on the murders?"

"Murders?" Joe asked. "You mean there's more than one?"

The chief looked at Joe and then at Katie, a confused expression on his face. "You mean you didn't hear about David Barclay's murder?"

"David Barclay is why we are here," Katie said. "Who else was killed?"

The chief leaned back in his chair. "Oh, I guess your news station missed a big story."

"I haven't worked for the news station in almost two years, except for a couple of freelance stories. Who else was killed?"

"Grace Ellington, the Mayor's daughter, was found dead the other day."

"The mayor's daughter? That's terrible. Did you catch the guy who did it?"

"We're not certain yet that she was murdered, but we think she was. If you no longer work for the news station, why are you here?"

"We're here to investigate Detective Barclay's murder," Katie said. "We believe Mitch Hartney is innocent and intend to prove it."

The chief laughed and shook his head. "You're wasting your time. I caught him red-handed."

"Did you see Mitch Hartney kill Detective Barclay?" Joe asked.

"Well, no, but I saw him standing over the body. And don't forget, this was days after he threatened to kill him."

"It was more like a week later," Katie said. "David, I mean, Detective Barclay, had stopped going to the hospital to see Jenna, which was the reason Mitch had threatened him. Since he stopped harassing Jenna, there was no reason for Mitch to kill him."

"That's just semantics. Listen, I'm very busy. It was a pleasure to see you again, Katie, but you need to go now."

"Not yet. We need to get some answers first," Katie said.

"I'm sure you do, but I don't have time to answer pointless questions."

Joe interrupted, saying, "You need to make time. Mitch Hartney deserves a fair trial, and the only way that will happen is if his legal representation has access to all the information that the police have."

"What do you mean by 'legal representation?'"

"He means Mitch's lawyer hired us to investigate the crime," Katie said.

"You've got to be kidding."

"It's true," Joe said. "If you don't want this case ending up as a mistrial, you need to share information with us."

The chief sighed. "Okay, fine. What do you want to know?"

"Tell us what happened from your point of view," Katie said.

"Well, it was Friday afternoon. Dave was working on the case involving the mayor's daughter. I left to speak with the mayor. That's when I saw Dave's body on the ground and Hartney standing over it."

"Did you see anyone else outside at the time?" Katie asked.

"No. There was nobody else around. I didn't know what happened at first, so I scanned the area but saw nothing unusual, except for the killer and his victim, of course."

"It seems you made up your mind that Mitch is guilty," Katie said. "I hope you will at least consider that his story might be true and investigate other possibilities."

The chief smiled and slowly shook his head. "You haven't changed a bit, Katie. You have that same tenacity that you had when we first met."

"How did you two meet?" Joe asked.

"I gave Katie her first ticket back when I was a street cop. Oh, you should have heard her try to argue her way out of it." He smiled as he relayed the story. "She blamed a tree branch for obscuring the stop sign."

"It was hanging down in front of the sign," Katie said defensively.

"It was the middle of winter," the chief said. "There were no leaves on the branch. It was just a few twigs in front of the sign."

Katie shrugged. "I figured it was worth a shot."

Joe laughed. "I can believe that story."

"Okay, okay. I've been good since then. That was my first and last ticket. Let's get back to why we are here. We will be investigating this case whether you like it or not, so I believe things will go smoother for both of us if you help us rather than hinder us."

The chief slowly nodded. "Okay. I will share information with you, but I think you're wasting your time."

"It's our time to waste," Katie said.

The chief got up, opened the door, and asked Cheryl to come into his office. When she did, he said, "Cheryl, until Katie and Joe here give up their little investigation, I want you to provide them with whatever information they need. Do you understand?"

Cheryl nodded. "Yes, Chief. No problem."

When they left the chief's office, Katie, Joe, and Cheryl stood in the reception area. Katie said. "The chief told us the mayor's daughter was killed. What do you know about that?"

"Oh, it was terrible. I knew her personally. They think she either fell into the river or someone killed her and dumped her body. She ended up in the marina, where a security guard found her."

"What day was that?" Joe asked.

"They found her body the same day that Dave was killed, but she probably died the night before. Dave was investigating her death before he was killed."

"This town hasn't had a murder in several years," Katie said. "What are the odds that two murders in less than twenty-four hours are a coincidence?"

"I don't know," Cheryl said. "I didn't give it much thought. I can't see how they are related."

"Maybe there's a serial killer in town," Katie said.

"In this town? I doubt it," Cheryl said. "People are far more likely to die from boredom."

"Maybe Grace's killer wanted to put a stop to the investigation," Joe said.

"Maybe," Cheryl said, "but if that's the case, the killer's an idiot because we will still investigate her death. He stopped nothing. In any case, we're not sure she didn't fall in the river and drown."

"When will they have the autopsy report back?" Joe asked.

"Do you mean for the mayor's daughter? Will you investigate that case, too?"

"It seems like a good place to start," Joe said.

"The autopsy was scheduled for this morning. We should know something very soon."

"Can you call us as soon as the results come in?" Katie asked.

"I can, but I think the chief only wanted me to help you with Mitch's case."

Katie shook her head. "No. He specifically said to provide us with whatever information we need, and we need that information."

Cheryl smiled. "That's right. He did say that, didn't he?"

Chapter 6

"What do you want to do now?" Joe asked when they left the police station.

"Let's talk to the mayor."

"The mayor? Tell me you're kidding. He just lost a child. Now is not a good time to be bothering him."

"It's been more than two days. How long should we wait?"

"I don't know. Maybe a year."

Katie laughed. "You're too funny, Joe." She took his hand and led him across the street.

City Hall was a block away. It wasn't called City Hall. Over the main entrance of the large, brick building were the words, "Municipal Building." Under that, in smaller letters, were "Minaka, Wisconsin."

Katie asked the receptionist if the mayor was available. She shook her head slowly and said, "I'm sorry. He'll be out for the rest of the week. Unfortunately, a tragedy occurred in his family."

"We know. We wanted to offer our condolences," Katie said.

"That's sweet. People have been leaving cards here if you want to do that."

"Okay. That's a good idea," Katie said. "We'll be back."

When they stepped outside, Joe asked, "Are you going to buy a card for the mayor?"

Katie stopped and looked at Joe. "Do you not know me by now? We're going to the mayor's house."

Katie walked quickly back toward the center of town, and Joe raced to catch up to her. "Are you crazy? We can't bother the man at his house at a time like this. How do you even know where he lives, anyway?"

Katie stopped again. "I know a lot of things about this town. I grew up here, remember? Plus, my dad and the mayor are friends."

"Friends? You mean like they hang out together, or do they just know each other and say hi sometimes?"

"They are not acquaintances, Joe, they are friends. The mayor opened the town's only hardware store around the same time my dad started at the high school as a maintenance man. Dad spent a lot of time at that hardware store, and the two of them became very close.

"Well, I guess if you know them, it won't hurt to go there and give our condolences."

"My thoughts, exactly."

They passed the town's center and continued walking for another block as snow started falling. There, on a corner lot at the crest of a steep hill, stood the mayor's home. From the front, it appeared to be a modest single-story bungalow with dark brown siding and a two-car garage. The other road that it sat on led down to the Mississippi River, a block or so away. From that road, the home's lower level appeared, as if it were built into the hill. A large deck extended from the top floor at the back of the house, offering a great view of the Mississippi River over the roof of the house that sat lower on the hill.

The driveway held two cars, parked side by side. Both cars were black. One was a Dodge Charger, probably belonging to the son. The other was a Chevy Impala. Next to the cars, on what used to be grass, was a boat on a trailer, covered for the winter. Katie remembered going out on the boat once when she was a teenager with her dad and the mayor. That was a good time.

Katie rang the bell. A middle-aged woman in a long black dress answered the door right away. She had shoulder-length dark hair with a few grey streaks. When she saw Katie, she smiled. Katie knew it was a sad smile, which made the reality of the situation sink in. "Katie!" the woman said. "It's good to see you again."

The two women hugged, and Katie said, "Hi, Connie. We just learned about Grace and wanted to offer our condolences."

"Come on inside," Connie said. "You must be cold."

Katie and Joe stepped inside. The kitchen was to their left, and the living room was ahead and to the right. To their immediate right was a staircase leading downstairs. The home was clean but not extravagant. It seemed average, like Katie's parents' house.

Mayor Ellington walked up the stairs after Joe closed the door behind him. He was a little taller than average with a thick frame. His hair was similar to his wife's, dark brown with gray streaks, but it was cut short. He wore a black suit with a white shirt and a blue tie. When he saw Katie, he smiled and said, "Katie, it's good to see you again."

They hugged, and Katie said, "Hi, Frank. We just heard what happened to Grace. I'm so sorry."

A young man in his mid-twenties came up the stairs. He resembled his father, but was much slimmer. He also wore a suit, but unlike his father, his tie was loose, and the top button of his shirt was undone. Frank put his hand on his son's arm and said, "You remember John."

"Of course," Katie said as she and John shook hands. She then introduced everyone to Joe.

"Did you come all the way out here because of Grace?" Frank asked.

"I'm sorry, we didn't," Katie said. "We learned what happened only this morning. We came to town to prove Mitch Hartney didn't kill David Barclay."

Frank shook his head. "This has been a terrible time not only for our family but for the entire town. What makes you think Hartney is innocent?"

"I know him well," Katie said. "He would never murder someone."

"Almost anyone is capable of killing under the right circumstances."

"Maybe killing, but not murder."

"Your dad told me you were settling into your job at the resort. He seemed to think now that you're raising a child, your investigating days were over."

"I don't know if the urge to find the truth will ever be over."

"It looks like you're dressed to go out," Joe said. "Are we interrupting?"

Frank shook his head. "No. We're going to the funeral home to make arrangements for Grace. It's not something any of us are in a hurry to do."

"I know this is a terrible time," Katie said, "but we want to look into what happened to Grace."

Frank studied her face for a moment and said, "I thought you said you were investigating the Barclay murder."

"We think they might be connected."

Frank was silent for a moment and said, "We don't know yet if Grace died accidentally or if someone killed her. If someone did kill her, I would do whatever it takes to find that person. With Detective Barclay dead, I'm not sure anyone on our police force has the experience of investigating a murder. You two have done it before. If you can help, I will support you in any way I can."

"I appreciate the vote of confidence," Katie said. "Do you know where Grace was that night?"

"No. We have no idea."

"Okay. We might have some questions for you later, but I think we've taken enough of your time. By the way, my parents don't know what has happened. They're at the resort taking care of our son, Joey. I'm sure once they learn, they will want to offer their support."

"Your parents are good people. Tell them to keep watching your little boy so you can keep doing what you do."

***

Katie's phone rang shortly after leaving the Ellingtons' house. It was Cheryl. She put the phone on speaker so Joe could hear. "Hi, Cheryl. What's up?"

"Grace's autopsy report came back. I thought you'd want to know what it says."

"Of course, we want to know. What does it say?"

"It says, 'Grace Ellington's cause of death is determined to be blunt force trauma to the skull. Contusions on the right cheek are consistent with a slap delivered shortly before death. The occipital laceration shows irregular tearing with embedded aggregate material consistent with concrete. The body entered the river postmortem.'"

"What does 'occipital' mean?" Katie asked.

"I think that has something to do with the back of the head," Joe said.

"Then that proves someone murdered her."

"It might have been an accident," Joe said. "The report says someone slapped her. That could have caused her to fall and hit her head on the concrete."

"If that's true," Cheryl said, "it was no accident."

"Good point," Joe said. "Do the police know anything about where she was the night she died?"

"I'm afraid not. The chief spoke with her parents, but they had no idea where she had been."

"Yeah. We were just at her parents' house," Katie said. "Thanks for the information, Cheryl."

After Katie hung up, Joe said, "If she fell on concrete, that means she was killed somewhere outside, probably in town. There's not much concrete out in the woods."

"That doesn't help much."

"No, but there are probably three places where she most likely was killed."

"Three? Where would those three places be?"

"Near her work, near her home, or near the killer's home."

"Since we don't know who the killer is, we can't look there, but we can certainly check out the other two places." Katie took out her phone and texted Cheryl, asking for Grace's home address and place of employment.

A few minutes later, Katie's phone beeped. She looked at it and read Cheryl's message. "Grace rented a house about a mile from here, and she worked at the bank near my parents' house. Let's get the car, and we can visit both places."

They walked back to the house and decided to use the washroom before continuing. On the way out, they heard the rooster crowing again.

"I thought roosters only crowed early in the morning," Katie said as she opened her car door.

"I don't know anything about roosters," Joe said. "Maybe this one's broken."

After they got into the car, Katie started the engine and said, "That's hard to believe. You've never lived around roosters during the last hundred years?"

"I've seen roosters, of course, but never lived near one. Before buying the resort, I lived a somewhat urban life."

Katie backed out of the driveway and headed toward the bank. "Yeah, but you spent forty years living in a cabin in the woods."

"True, but I never raised chickens or any other animal, for that matter, except for occasional pets. I prefer to find animals in nature."

"I suppose that's the photographer in you."

The bank was only a block away, so they arrived there quickly. It was a small, single-story building on a corner lot. It was relatively new, having been built less than five years earlier when Katie lived in Milwaukee. A friendly teller greeted them when they walked inside.

"Hello," Katie said. "We'd like to speak to the branch manager."

"Of course," the teller said. "Have a seat. He'll be with you shortly."

Five minutes later, an older man, perhaps in his early sixties, greeted them. He had short, graying hair and wore wire-rim glasses and a charcoal-gray suit. He smiled and said, "Hello. I'm Tim Williams, the branch manager. How can I help you today?"

"Hi, Tim," Katie said. "My name's Katie Novak, and this is my husband, Joe. I first want to say we are sorry for your loss."

"Thank you. We were all very saddened about what happened to Grace. Is that why you're here?"

"Yes. We're investigating her death, and we're hoping you could answer a few questions for us."

"Aren't you two a little young to be investigators?"

Joe looked at Katie and said, "I think we might have an age discrimination case here."

Tim shifted on his feet and cleared his throat. "I, uh, I didn't mean anything by it."

Katie slapped Joe's arm and said, "Don't mind my husband, he thinks he's funny sometimes."

Joe smiled, and Tim exhaled a sigh of relief. "You had me worried for a minute. People are sue happy these days."

"We are not like that, and for your information, we are older than you think," Katie said.

"So, did someone hire you to investigate Grace's death?"

"We were hired to investigate the death of Detective Barclay, but there is a possibility the two murders are related," Joe said.

"Was Grace murdered? The last we heard, the police didn't know yet."

"We recently learned that she died before going into the river," Katie said.

Tim slowly shook his head. "Why would anyone want to kill such a lovely young woman? And smart, too. Do you know she was the youngest loan officer to ever work at this bank?" He paused and added, "Why do you think her murder and the detective's murder are related?"

"We don't know that they are, but two murders in less than a day seem suspicious," Katie said.

"Do you think the guy they have in custody killed Grace, too?"

"Definitely not," Katie said. "We believe the man they have in custody is innocent, and we are here to prove it."

"Okay," Tim said slowly. "How can I help you?"

"Do you know what Grace did after work the night she was killed?" Joe asked.

"No, I'm afraid not. She didn't talk much about her personal life. Gina might know more. She's the teller you talked to when you came in."

"Do you mind if we speak with her?" Katie asked.

"Not at all," Tim said. He looked up and saw that there were no customers inside the bank, so he motioned for Gina to come over. When she arrived, Tim introduced her to Katie and Joe, and then he returned to his office.

Gina was young, around the same age as Grace, with blue eyes and long, blond hair. She smiled and asked, "What can I do for you?"

"Hi, Gina," Katie said. "We are investigators looking into what happened to Grace. Were you and she friends?"

73

"Yes. I would say so. We didn't hang out after work, but we got along very well here. She could always make me laugh."

"Do you know what she did after work the day she was killed?" Katie asked.

"She told me she had a date."

Katie and Joe looked at each other, then Joe asked, "A date? With whom?"

"I don't know. She told me she ran into someone she used to know."

"Do you know where she knew him from?" Joe asked.

"She didn't say. She believed it was bad luck to discuss a date before it happened. She said she would tell me the next day. I guess she was wrong, huh? Maybe it was bad luck not to talk about it."

"I don't think luck was responsible for what happened," Joe said.

"Where did she run into this guy?" Katie asked.

"She said she saw him before work, so I assume it was at the coffee shop. She stops there every morning for a coffee."

"Where does she get coffee?" Katie asked.

"Over at the Minaka Perk."

"Did you tell the police that information?" Joe asked.

"No. I haven't seen the police since Grace died."

"You mean no one came here to question Grace's coworkers?" Katie asked, a look of amazement on her face.

"No, but with that detective getting killed, I suppose they have a lot on their plate."

Katie and Joe looked at each other, then Katie said, "Thanks so much for your time, Gina." She reached into her purse, removed a business card, and handed it to her. "Please call if you think of anything else that might help."

Joe looked surprised but said nothing until they got outside. "Where did you get those business cards?"

"I ordered them a while ago."

"Let me see one."

Katie stopped walking, took another card from her purse, and handed it to Joe. He looked at it and said, "It says, 'Katie Novak, Freelance Reporter.' I thought you were done with all that."

"I never said I was done with anything. My old station is willing to pay me for freelance work, so why not take advantage of that when a story comes up?"

"Well, that's fine, I guess, but you should have told me about the cards."

"I love you, Joe, but you can be overprotective sometimes. I figured you would poo-poo the idea."

"Poo-poo?"

"Yeah. You know, when someone tells you your idea is bad."

"I don't think keeping your options open is a bad idea."

"Really? You're not afraid I'm going to get kidnapped by some crazed killer that we are investigating?"

"I think the odds of getting kidnapped three times are astronomically low."

Katie was silent for several seconds and finally said. "Who are you and what did you do with my husband?"

Joe laughed. "I'm still going to worry about you, but I realized that you are who you are, and trying to make you something you're not will only make us both unhappy."

"Okay, wait. Just to be clear, are you saying you are willing to go out and look for murders to investigate rather than wait for them to fall into our laps?"

"No. I didn't say that, exactly."

"You used the word, 'exactly.' That means there is some wiggle room." Katie hugged Joe. "You're the best husband ever."

Joe shook his head. "I need to learn when to keep my mouth shut."

When they returned to the car, Joe asked, "Where is this Minaka Perk?"

"It's about halfway between here and Grace's house," Katie said as she started the engine.

***

They arrived at the coffee shop three minutes later. It was on the main road into town, in a small building on a corner lot that appeared to have once been a home. It had white siding, brown trim, and a steep, red shingle roof. There were spots in the front for parallel parking and a small parking lot in the back. The building had no drive-thru.

The snow was still coming down in flurries as they entered the coffee shop. Inside, the atmosphere was cozy, with soft lighting, old hardwood floors, and mismatched furniture. The aroma of coffee and pastries filled the air.

Katie and Joe walked past several small wooden tables and chairs, as well as more comfortable cushioned armchairs. There were about a dozen people inside. Some sat together on the armchairs while others sat alone at the tables with their laptops open. An old James Taylor song played softly through the speakers, adding a gentle rhythm to the low hum of conversation.

Since no one was in line, they stepped up to the counter. A woman, perhaps in her mid-fifties, with her hair tied in a bun and covered with a hair net, smiled and said, "Hi. What can I get for you?"

Katie noticed her nametag and said, "Good morning, Lisa. We need some information. We are investigating the death of Grace Ellington."

"Oh, I was heartbroken when I heard what happened to her. Are you cops? You look a bit young."

"No. We are private investigators," Katie said, ignoring the comment about their age.

"We heard Grace was a regular visitor here," Joe said.

"Oh yes. She would come every morning before work for an iced coffee. It didn't matter if it was ten degrees outside."

"A coworker of hers told us that she met someone here the morning that she died," Katie said.

The woman thought for a moment and said, "Now that you mention it, she did stop and talk to a young man for a few minutes before she left."

"What did this man look like?" Katie asked.

"Oh, I think he was young, maybe Grace's age. I don't know. At my age, everyone under forty looks young. He was also taller than average." She looked at Joe. "He was about your height. Maybe a little taller. I'm not sure. I was busy and only saw them for a brief moment. He also had straight, brown hair like yours, but his face seemed a little rounder."

"Have you ever seen him before?" Joe asked.

"He looked vaguely familiar, but he wasn't a regular."

"Do you know who he is?" Katie asked.

"No. I'm sorry. I live in Trempealeau, so I don't know many people in this town unless they're regulars. Do you think this man killed Grace?"

"It's possible," Katie said, "but everything is speculation until we learn more."

"Do you know what kind of vehicle he drove?" Joe asked.

"I'm afraid not. I can't see the parking lot from here."

"Do you have cameras?" Joe asked.

The woman shook her head. "Nope. I never saw a need to have them installed until now."

Katie removed a business card from her purse and handed it to the woman. "Thanks so much. Please call us if you think of anything else or if you see the man again."

The woman looked at the card and said, "Of course. If that man did kill Grace, I hope you find him."

Chapter 7

The snowfall had stopped by the time they stepped out of the coffee shop, but a thin layer still blanketed the roads as they made their way to Grace Ellington's house. She lived on the edge of town in a small, single-story ranch-style house with teal siding and white trim. Katie pulled into the driveway and parked behind an older model Toyota Camry. "Her car is still in the driveway," Joe said. "Whoever killed her must have picked her up."

"That pretty much confirms that she had a date."

They got out of the car and looked around. A row of tall shrubs separated the house from its neighbor on the left. There were no homes across the street or to the right. Joe shook his head. "It's unlikely anyone would have seen who picked her up."

Several stepping stones lay on the ground between the driveway and the sidewalk leading to the house. When they reached the sidewalk, Katie pushed the snow away with her foot, exposing the concrete. "Did you know that about a quarter of all murders happen at the victim's own home?"

"Really? I thought I was the one who knew all the useless trivia."

"Oh, you're still the useless trivia champ, but this isn't useless trivia. Considering that Grace died after hitting her head on concrete, I think there's a good chance this is where she died."

"I agree," Joe said before heading back to the car.

"What are you doing, Joe?"

"You'll see," he said as he opened the trunk and removed the ice scraper. It was the kind that had a brush on one end. He walked back to where Katie stood and started brushing the snow off the sidewalk. When he got close to the steps leading up to the porch, he stopped. "Look at this."

Katie looked down and saw an oval-shaped area that was slightly larger than her hand and darker than the surrounding area. "Is that blood?"

"I think so. It looks like someone tried to wash it away with water, but he must not have had very much."

"Do you think the police know about this?"

"I don't think the police know much about anything."

"I'm sure losing their only detective has something to do with that," Katie said.

"I suppose we should tell them what we found."

"Yes, but then the chief will get on our case about interfering with his investigation, and we don't have a legitimate reason to be investigating Grace Ellington's murder, at least not as far as he is concerned."

Joe nodded slowly. "I guess we can keep this to ourselves for now. Let's see what else we can learn before we say anything."

***

When they got in the car, Katie said, "Let's get something to eat. I'm hungry."

"Or we can pick up some food at the store, and I can make a nice lunch for us," Joe said.

"That will take too long. It will be time for dinner before we eat."

"Okay. Whatever you want, my dear."

Katie looked at Joe, smiled, and put a hand on his leg. She knew he would much rather cook something than go out to eat. A couple of times a month, they would dress up and go to a fancy restaurant for dinner. She understood Joe only did it for her, but he never complained. It was moments like those when she felt that the day she met Joe was the luckiest day of her life.

That day was a little less lucky for Joe because she hit him with her car and nearly killed him. Fortunately, Joe was blessed with the ability to consciously direct his body to heal itself. By the following day, it was as if the injuries never happened.

"How about we go out for lunch, and afterwards we can get what we need so you can cook us a nice dinner," Katie suggested.

"Okay," Joe said. "That's a great idea."

They chose a pizza restaurant, and they each ordered two slices of cheese pizza and a bottle of water. Katie was tempted to order a soda, but she didn't like the look Joe gave her when she made unhealthy choices. She couldn't understand why Joe always wanted to do healthy things. He was the Healer, after all. He could heal from the adverse effects of things like a jelly donut if he wanted to, but he preferred to eat salads and bought organic meats and produce whenever possible. To her, it seemed silly to have such a wonderful gift and not take advantage of it, but she chose not to question it. If Joe were to die before her, which was unlikely, it would be good for her to have healthy habits since he would no longer be there to keep her well.

"Maybe we should tell Cheryl what we found," Katie said as they waited for their food.

"Don't you think she will feel obligated to tell the chief?"

"I have an idea about that. If we tell her when she's off duty, she may not feel as obligated."

Joe nodded. "Okay, we'll do that."

After lunch, Katie called Cheryl and learned she was out on patrol. They agreed to meet at Katie's parents' house after Cheryl's shift ended at three. That gave them enough time to go shopping for food.

There was a small market in town, but they decided to drive fifteen minutes away to the nearest supermarket so Joe could get all the ingredients he needed. The weather had warmed to above freezing, and the small amount of snow on the roads had melted.

While at the supermarket, Joe also picked up some items for a few other meals, including breakfast, anticipating that they would be there for more than a day. Katie's parents, expecting to be gone for a week, left their refrigerator mostly empty.

After Katie and Joe returned to the house and put the groceries away, they sat on the sofa together. "We have some time before Cheryl gets here," Joe said.

"I want to see how Joey is doing," Katie said as she picked up her phone and started a video call with her mom.

Her mom's face appeared on the screen as she said, "Hi Katie. How's the investigation going?"

"We're hopeful, but we haven't learned anything useful yet. How's Joey been treating you? We want to say hi to him."

"Oh, Joey has been a handful, but in a good way. Dad wore him out today, or maybe the other way around." She turned the phone so Katie and Joe could see Karl asleep on the sofa with Joey asleep on his lap.

"That's too cute, Mom. When he wakes up, tell him Mommy and Daddy love him, and we'll be home soon."

"Will do, Honey. You get back to your investigation and don't worry about a thing."

When she hung up the phone, Joe said, "Perhaps this is a good time for a healing session."

Katie held Joe's hand. "It's always a good time for that."

What Joe called a "healing session" was something Katie loved more than anything else in her life, other than her family. It was an indescribable connection that only a handful of people in the world had ever experienced. When they were connected, it was as if they were one person. They still had different minds and different thoughts, but their physical feelings were identical. It was like a feeling of intimacy, but at a much deeper level.

When Joe learned he could heal others, those people could feel what he felt, which was dangerous because if people knew of his unique abilities, his freedom might be in jeopardy. He had since learned how to prevent people from feeling what he felt. Nevertheless, he allowed Katie, as well as his family, to feel everything.

After meeting Katie and sharing his secret with her, Joe asked her to help him investigate the truth about his origins. Together, they uncovered stories of other Healers who had once lived in the small Croatian village where his parents came from. They learned that these Healers could heal people through a simple touch. Joe was unaware he had that ability and tried to learn to use it, but failed. It wasn't until Katie was near death that he learned the secret. Out of desperation, he discovered he could connect to Katie by thinking of her as an extension of himself rather than as a separate person.

"Your muscles are a little tense," Joe said shortly after connecting to Katie. "What's wrong?"

"Nothing's wrong. I don't feel any tension."

"Are you worried about Joey?"

"No. My parents can take care of him. I'm not worried."

Joe was silent for a few seconds and then said, "That's not true. You are worried about him."

"Okay, fine. You're right. I'm a little worried."

"It's normal to be worried, but it's not healthy. Can you feel what it's doing to you?"

Katie paused and concentrated on what was happening inside her body. She compared it to Joe's body and said, "You're right. My muscles are a little tense, and my heart rate and blood pressure are higher than normal."

"What else?"

Katie concentrated. "I feel a high amount of a certain hormone."

"That's a stress hormone. You need to slow down its production."

Almost two years earlier, Joe was shot in the back. The bullet punctured his lung, causing difficulty in breathing. He couldn't concentrate on breathing and healing at the same time, so he connected to Katie, and she became the Healer. Now she was learning things that Joe knew almost instinctively. She was learning how to heal herself.

When the session was over, Katie said, "You were quite confident I wasn't telling the truth when I said I wasn't worried about Joey. How did you know?"

"I didn't know for sure, but I felt some subtle changes in your heart rate and breathing. Changes that are not normal for you."

"Great. Now I have a lie detector for a husband."

"I confess, I'm a little worried too. I've just learned to control the stress response."

"We're both a mess. What will we do if we have another child?"

Joe looked surprised at the comment. "Another child. Are you ready for that?"

"I don't know, Joe. Is anybody ready for another child?"

"We haven't talked about it. Would you like to have another baby?"

Katie was silent for several seconds and finally said, "I think I would like a little girl. I want someone I can teach about fashion, and makeup, and boys…"

"Wait! Boys? Aren't we getting a little ahead of ourselves?"

"What do you think, Joe? Can you use your ability to make the next one a girl?"

Joe shook his head. "I'm afraid those little buggers are out of my control."

Katie sighed. "Well, it was just a thought."

***

Cheryl arrived at the house a few minutes after three, still dressed in her police uniform, but driving her personal vehicle. After the customary greetings, Katie invited her to sit in the living room with her and Joe.

"Have the police learned anything new about either of the murders?" Katie asked.

Cheryl shook her head. "I hate to tell you, but nobody is investigating David's murder. The chief is convinced that Mitch killed him. As far as Grace's murder, we've learned nothing important since we last spoke."

"I would think the mayor would be putting pressure on the chief to get answers," Joe said.

"He is, and the chief is putting pressure on Ken, I mean, Sergeant Daniels. He's in charge of the case now, but he's stretched thin with his other duties. Plus, he has never investigated a murder before. Nobody in the department has, not even the chief."

"Maybe he should get some outside help," Katie said. "I'm sure the Sheriff's department has some experienced investigators."

"I suggested that to Ken, but he told me never to mention that in front of the chief. I guess asking for help is a threat to his ego."

"That's a man for you," Katie said.

"Hey!" Joe said. "You can't lump all men into the same box."

"Really? When's the last time you couldn't do something important on your own and asked for help?"

"Just the other day, I couldn't get the printer to work and asked for your help."

"That's because my grandma knows more about computers than you do."

"Both your grandmas are dead."

"And still they know more than you, but I'm not talking about things you are bad at. When is the last time you asked for help with something you were good at but still couldn't do it?"

Joe thought for a moment and said, "What about that time in Milwaukee when I was shot and needed your help?"

"Oh, yeah," Katie said. "I guess that qualifies."

Cheryl looked puzzled. "Getting shot isn't something that people are good at."

"Joe is good at staying healthy."

"No one can expect to stay healthy after getting shot."

"Exactly," Katie said. Realizing they had brought up a topic that they shouldn't have, she tried to change the subject. "We found what might be blood on the sidewalk near Grace's house, but we don't want to upset the chief by telling him about it. I'm sure he will tell us to stick with Mitch's case."

"No doubt," Cheryl said. "Ken was heading over to Grace's house as I got off work. Maybe I'll go meet him there before going home and make sure he notices the sidewalk."

"Good idea," Katie said. "If we can confirm that was blood we saw, it would at least give us a place of death."

***

After Cheryl left, Joe said, "You know, the mayor was okay with you looking into Grace's death. Why don't we tell the chief that?"

"We will if we get backed into a corner, but it's probably best to stay off the chief's radar if we can."

A few minutes later, Jenna called. When Katie saw her name on the screen, she showed Joe the phone, then answered it. "Hi Jenna," she said. "Is everything okay?"

"Yes and no. I just wanted to let you know Sophia is feeling much better. It's hard to believe, but her sore throat is completely gone, and her temperature has returned to normal. Tell Joe he's a miracle worker."

Katie looked at Joe and smiled. "He is amazing. There's no doubt about that. What's the bad news?"

"The judge set Mitch's bail at half a million dollars. There's no way we can afford that."

"Oh, that's tough," Katie said. "Hopefully, we'll find the real killer soon."

"Did you guys learn anything new about David's murder?"

"We're following a couple of leads, but nothing concrete yet."

"Well, just keep doing what you're doing. I'm sure you'll find something."

"Yeah, of course we will," Katie said, not sure if she believed her own words.

When Katie finished the call, she sat on the sofa with her laptop. Joe sat next to her and watched. After a couple of minutes, he asked, "What are you looking for?"

"I'm looking at a satellite view of the town. I want to know where someone might go to dump a body in the river."

Joe looked at her screen as she zoomed in on an area of town and said, "Wow! That is really something. Is that live?"

Katie looked up at Joe in amazement. "Live? No. It's not live."

She zoomed in on the image of the town near the Mississippi River. She switched to a street view and followed the street north until there were no more houses. She saw an area near the river devoid of trees. "I think I found something."

Joe looked at the image on the computer screen. "That looks like a perfect place to dump a body."

"It doesn't help us. There is nothing out there that would have a camera."

"What about the houses along the road a little south of there?"

"A lot of vehicles drive on that road. Without knowing an exact time, videos of cars going by would be of no use to us. We're back at square one."

"Maybe, but we know Grace was out on a date that night. Maybe we can find someone who saw them."

"Let's hope we do. I don't want to fail Jenna."

"Right now, I think you should put your computer away and take your mind off the case for a while. Sometimes it's easier to think after you give your mind a break. I'll get dinner started. You can watch TV if you want. I know you probably miss that."

"I actually don't," Katie said. "I'd rather hang out with you in the kitchen."

The kitchen had a counter that separated it from the dining room. On the other side of the counter stood two short barstools. Katie sat on one of the stools and watched Joe work. "What are you making for dinner?" she asked.

"It's called Chicken Paprikash."

Katie raised an eyebrow, "I never heard of that. What is it?"

"It's a Hungarian dish," he said. "It's chicken simmered in a paprika sauce with a little sour cream. I learned it from my son's wife. Her mother would make it at the start of winter."

"I hate to break it to you, but we are in the middle of winter."

"Technically, winter started three weeks ago."

"Don't get technical. Winter starts when you can see your breath, and that was way more than three weeks ago."

"Do you want me to make something else?"

"No, no. Carry on."

Joe set a cutting board on the counter and sliced chicken into chunks. Then, unfamiliar with the kitchen, he rummaged through several cabinets before Katie said, "If you're looking for a frying pan, they're in the cabinet next to the stove."

Joe opened the cabinet, found a large cast-iron pan, and placed it on the stove. He turned on the burner, added a little oil, and carefully placed the chicken pieces into the pan.

Katie began flipping through a gossip magazine that was on the counter while Joe cooked the chicken. He took out a large onion and asked Katie if she wanted to dice it.

"Never again," Katie said.

"Just because you cut yourself one time is no reason to give up on dicing onions."

"You're right, Joe, it's not, but having a husband who cooks for me is a great reason."

Joe smiled and shook his head. "I think I spoil you too much."

Without looking up from her magazine, Katie said, "You think so, huh? Try spoiling me less and see what happens."

Ten minutes later, Joe put a cover on the pan and said, "This needs to cook for at least forty-five minutes."

Katie put the magazine down and said, "Do you remember what we used to do while dinner was cooking before Joey was born?"

Joe smiled, "Oh, are you suggesting we revive an old tradition?"

Katie got up from her stool, took Joe's hand, and said, "Come with me, old man," before leading him upstairs to the bedroom.

Chapter 8

The next morning, Joe and Katie arranged to meet Cheryl at the police station early. They walked there again, arriving a short time before eight. Cheryl met them in the lobby and ushered them back to her desk.

"Did you and Sergeant Daniels find the blood on the sidewalk yesterday?" Katie asked.

"We sure did. Believe it or not, Ken had noticed it before I arrived. I was worried I would have to show it to him. I didn't want to deflate his ego."

"Do you think that would have bothered him?" Joe asked.

"Would it bother you if you were in his shoes?" Cheryl asked.

Joe shook his head. "No. Maybe when I was young, but not now."

"What do you mean when you were young? What are you now?"

"I think Joe means when he was a kid," Katie said.

"Yes," Joe said. "When I was in high school, I knew everything. Not so much now."

Cheryl nodded. "It seems you have gained some wisdom at a much younger age than most men do."

"I can always count on Joe to either be wise or a wise ass," Katie said, which got a chuckle out of Cheryl.

"Anyway," Cheryl said, "we sent some samples to the lab and should know if it's human blood by tomorrow. DNA tests will take longer."

"Did you learn if David uncovered any leads in Grace's murder before he died?" Katie asked.

"Ken is here. Let's ask him."

Cheryl led Katie and Joe to the other side of the room, where they found Ken at his desk, filling out a report on his computer. Cheryl interrupted him, saying, "Hey, Ken. Do you have a minute?

Ken swiveled in his chair, looked at Cheryl, and said, "What's up, Cheryl?"

Cheryl was standing in front of Katie and Joe, so she stepped aside and said, "You remember Katie, don't you?"

When Ken saw Katie, his eyes lit up, and he said, "Of course. It's been a long time. You look great. I heard you were in town investigating Dave's murder."

"Yes, we are." Katie put her hand on Joe's arm and said, "This is my husband, Joe."

They shook hands, and Ken said, "Nice to meet you, Joe."

"We're here to find out what you learned about Grace Ellington's death," Katie said.

"The mayor's daughter? I thought you were here investigating Dave's murder."

"We are, but we think there may be a connection," Katie said.

"No. There's no connection. We know who killed Dave, and his motive has nothing to do with Grace Ellington."

"We are here under the assumption that Mitch Hartney is telling the truth and someone else killed the detective," Joe said. "We only ask that you keep an open mind. If we're wrong, then you will not only lose nothing, but it would also make your case against Mitch Hartney stronger."

"How will it make our case stronger?" Ken asked.

"It will make your case stronger because then you will be able to tell a jury you looked at every angle."

Ken nodded. "Okay. I can keep an open mind. Tell me why you think these cases are related."

"First of all," Katie said, "the coincidence is too great. We haven't had a murder in town in years, but now we have two in less than a day. Second, Dave was working on Grace's murder when he was killed. What if her killer wanted to squash the investigation?"

"That doesn't make sense. You can't squash the investigation of the murder of the mayor's daughter."

"What if the detective had evidence?" Katie asked. "Maybe the killer took it from him."

Ken slowly nodded. "I'm not saying I believe any of this, but I can see where that might make sense."

"So, can we work together on this?" Katie asked.

Ken shook his head. "No. We can't work together; however, I'm not opposed to sharing information with you when appropriate."

Katie smiled. "So, what did Dave learn before he died?"

"As far as I can tell, nothing. He died before making it back inside the station. We checked his car but found nothing. We tried to check his phone, but it's locked, and we can't get into it. The chief said Dave found a man's ring at the crime scene, engraved with a single letter. He said it was a 'W.' We didn't find the ring on him or in his car."

"So, you see? There is a connection," Katie said. "Whoever killed Dave took the ring. Why do you think he would have done that if he didn't also kill Grace?"

Cheryl nodded, but Ken shook his head. "I don't know. There could be a dozen reasons why the ring was missing."

"Okay," Katie said. "Name one."

"Well, I don't know. Maybe it fell out of his pocket."

"That's ridiculous, and you know it," Katie said.

"Maybe it is, but if you are right, there is a good chance Mitch Hartney has two murders on his hands."

Katie was silent for several seconds, feeling she had walked into a trap. She then replied, "But you said earlier Mitch had no connection to Grace."

"That's what I thought," Ken said, "but now we need to look into the possibility."

Katie looked at Joe, silently pleading for him to say something helpful. "What was Grace's estimated time of death?" Joe asked.

"According to the medical examiner, she died sometime between eight and ten o'clock that night," Ken said.

Joe looked at Katie. "Call Jenna and ask her where Mitch was that night."

"Good idea," Katie said and called her friend. When she answered, Katie put it on speaker and said, "Hi Jenna. Joe and I are at the police station with Cheryl and Sergeant Ken. We need to ask you where Mitch was the night Grace Ellington died."

"What? Why do you want to know that? Do the police think he killed her, too?"

"The topic did come up," Katie said. "We just want to confirm he was home with you so we can clear this up."

Jenna was silent for several seconds before saying, "He worked late that night."

Katie turned to Joe, a shocked look on her face. She looked back at the phone. "What time did he get home?"

"I don't know. Nine. Nine thirty. Something like that."

Katie put her hand over her mouth. She didn't know what to say. Joe took the phone from Katie and finished the conversation. "Thank you, Jenna. We'll talk later. We have to go."

"Wait a minute...," Jenna said as Joe hung up.

A smile appeared on Ken's face. "Well, Katie, it seems the chief was mistaken. The letter on the ring wasn't a 'W' after all, but an 'M' for 'Mitch.' It looks like you just helped us find Grace's killer. Thanks for the assistance."

***

"Stupid! Stupid! Stupid!" Katie said as she and Joe walked out of the police station. "We came here to help Mitch, and I just made it worse for him."

"It's not your fault," Joe said. "I'm the one who suggested calling Jenna."

"Yeah, but I put Mitch on their radar, which means it was only a matter of time before they found out he was not at home that night."

"I'm sure the police would have eventually looked at him for Grace's murder, even without your input."

"Maybe, but I still feel terrible. How will I face Jenna now? What am I going to tell her?"

Katie's phone rang. She looked at it and showed Joe that Jenna was calling. "I guess we'll know soon," Joe said.

Katie answered the phone. "Hi Jenna," she said sheepishly.

"What the hell was that all about? Are you still at the police station?"

"No. We just left."

"Do the police think Mitch killed Grace, too?"

"I'm sorry, Jenna. It's all my fault. I wanted to convince Ken Daniels that the person who murdered Grace also murdered David. I thought we could at least cast doubt on Mitch's guilt by giving the police another suspect. I had no idea Mitch was out late that night."

"He wasn't out late. He was working. Are you having doubts now about Mitch's innocence?"

"Doubts? No. Not at all, but now we need to clear him of two murders."

After a long pause, Jenna said, "Just do what you do best. I have to go."

Katie was about to say something, but the line went dead. She put her phone in her pocket and said, "She's pissed, and I don't blame her."

"She's upset. Give her time. She might be having doubts about her husband's innocence. That alone could devastate a person. This is a time when she needs her best friend more than ever."

"This is a time when she thinks her best friend is causing her more grief, and she would be right."

"I'm sure she will eventually realize it wasn't your fault, Katie. She'll come around."

"I hope so."

"I'm going to play Devil's Advocate and ask if Mitch may be guilty?"

Katie stopped walking and looked at Joe. "Don't tell me you think Mitch is guilty, now?"

"No. I don't think that, but I do think we need to prepare ourselves for the possibility that he might be guilty."

"The 'possibility' that he 'might' be guilty," Katie repeated, stressing *possibility* and *might*. "You're really hedging your bets here, Mister. I think you need to pick a side."

"We are here to prove Mitch is innocent, and that is what we are going to do," Joe said.

Katie said nothing. She just linked arms with Joe, and they continued to walk to the restaurant. It was the same restaurant where they had breakfast the previous morning. After they ordered, Katie said, "I think we need to go see Mitch again today."

"I agree," Joe said. "How do we arrange that?"

"I don't know. Jenna did it last time. I should call her, but maybe I should wait for her to cool down first."

"Waiting won't change anything. Call her now."

Katie sighed and took out her phone. She called Jenna and told her that they wanted to speak to Mitch again. She said she was planning on going there and invited Katie and Joe to come along.

"See? She's over it already," Joe said when Katie hung up.

"I hope so, or this will be an uncomfortable ride."

***

After breakfast, they walked to Jenna's house. It was nearly the same distance from the restaurant as Katie's parents' house. Katie rang the bell, and after a few seconds, Jenna opened the door and invited them inside.

"I'm so sorry," Katie said when they stepped inside. "I was trying to help Mitch, not hurt him."

Jenna hugged Katie. "No. I'm the one who should be sorry. I know you and Joe are trying to help. It wasn't your fault. I would have told you about Mitch coming home late that night, but I didn't think it was relevant."

"I'm sure it's not relevant," Katie said, "but now the police have another reason to think Mitch is guilty."

"I don't know about you two, but I'm eager to hear what Mitch has to say," Joe said.

"Of course," Jenna said. "Let me get my keys. We can take my car."

Katie sat in the front next to Jenna while Joe climbed into the back seat behind Katie. As they backed out of the driveway, Joe looked around and said, "This is so roomy. I'm not used to driving in a real car."

"We don't need any wise-ass comments from the back," Katie said.

Joe smiled and leaned back in his seat. He took pleasure in occasionally teasing Katie about the small size of her Mini Cooper, which she relished. It was the first car she bought brand new, and she took pride in keeping it in prime condition.

When they got in to see Mitch, Jenna spoke to him for a couple of minutes and then told him Katie and Joe had a few questions. Katie exchanged chairs with Jenna, and Joe stood behind her. "Jenna said you worked late the night Grace Ellington was murdered," Katie said. "What were you doing at work?"

"Is that why you are here? Do you think I had something to do with Grace's death?"

"No, but the police will be investigating the possibility," Katie said.

"Oh, great! As if I didn't have enough problems. I can't catch a break."

"It's fine," Katie said. "If we can prove you didn't kill Grace, that will give the police another suspect in David's murder."

Mitch was silent for several seconds and said, "I don't know how to prove it. I was at work alone."

"Do you have cameras in your office?" Joe asked.

"No, but the alarm company would have a report of when I set the alarm that night."

"What time was that?" Katie asked.

"I'm not certain. It was some time after nine."

Katie looked at Joe, who said, "It's not enough. The police will just say you returned and shut off the alarm after you killed Grace. Did anyone see you leave?"

"Not that I know of. There's nothing open downtown that late except Jack's Pub, and that's out of sight of my office."

"Did you make a phone call from your office that evening?" Katie asked. "If so, maybe your phone records would prove you were there."

Mitch thought for a moment and said, "No. I didn't talk to anyone. I do remember the phone ringing once, but I let the voicemail answer it."

"That's too bad," Katie said.

"Why were you working late that night?" Joe asked.

"It was a busy week. I needed to prepare for a custody case the following morning."

"Did you win it?" Katie asked.

"I don't know if anyone wins in custody battles, but we achieved our objective."

"Of course," Katie said. "Is there anything else you can think of that might help us?"

Mitch shook his head. "I'm afraid not."

"Okay, Mitch. Don't worry. We'll figure something out."

When the conversation was over, and they stepped outside of the visitation room, Joe said, "I was thinking about the last case we worked on. Remember, we were able to find where someone was from their phone's GPS?"

"I already considered that, Joe, but the police will only assume he left his phone in his office."

"I suppose you're right."

"That was a good idea, though. I'm impressed that you are thinking about high-tech solutions."

"I may not be tech-savvy like you, but I'm not blind to technology either."

"I know, Joe. Just last week, you suggested that I fax a document to someone. That's progress."

"Very funny," Joe said.

Jenna laughed. "You guys are too much. I think it's refreshing that Joe is more like Daniel Boone than Bill Gates."

Katie looked at Joe and smiled. "He probably knew Daniel Boone."

"Oh, you are a load of laughs today," Joe said.

"I don't get it," Jenna said.

"Katie teases me because I'm older than she is."

Jenna looked Joe up and down and said, "Seriously. I thought you were like twenty-four."

"According to my license, I'm twenty-eight, but they made a mistake and printed the wrong year, and I have not been in a hurry to correct it. My birthday is actually more than three months before Katie's." That was technically correct, but Joe left out the fact that he was born in 1916, while Katie was born in 1994.

"Well, you both look great for being over thirty."

On the way back to town, they stopped for lunch. The restaurant had a large U-shaped bar in the center of the room. They sat at a table near a window overlooking a busy street. When they opened their menus, Katie said, "This place has the best hamburgers in the county."

They all ordered burgers, and while they waited for their food, Jenna said, "I'm worried. How will we prove Mitch is innocent with all this evidence against him?"

"There is still so much we don't know yet," Joe said. "That's a good thing. It means the more we learn, the better things will be."

"What if you learn things that make Mitch look more guilty?"

A surprised look came over Katie's face. "Really, Jenna? Are you starting to worry that he might be guilty?"

"No. Of course not. I'm just not naive enough to think that because he is my husband and I love him, he is incapable of doing anything bad. What if I don't know him like I think I do?"

"Don't do this to yourself," Katie said. "We spoke with a woman at the coffee shop who saw Grace Ellington with a man whom she described as someone who looked different than Mitch. We think that man killed Grace."

"Just because Grace talked to a man at a coffee shop doesn't mean he's the killer."

"Her coworker also said that she had a date with a man she met that morning. We believe he's the same man."

"Really?" Jenna asked. "If that's true, you need to find that man."

"I agree, but we don't have much to go on yet," Katie said.

"Did David learn anything before he died?" Jenna asked.

"Nobody knows," Katie said. "Apparently, he found a man's ring, but it conveniently disappeared."

"A ring? What kind of ring?"

"A ring with a letter engraved on it," Katie said. "The chief thinks it was a 'W.' Ken, the police sergeant, suggested it was an 'M.'"

"Did Mitch have a ring like that?" Joe asked.

"No. Mitch didn't care for jewelry. He only wore his wedding ring."

"Well, that's evidence in Mitch's favor," Joe said.

Jenna nodded and smiled. It was more of a half-smile, but Katie was happy to see it. She touched Jenna's arm and said, "We will figure this out."

Chapter 9

Jenna needed to get home before her kids returned from school, so after lunch, she dropped Katie and Joe off at Katie's parents' house.

Katie went straight to the sofa, leaned back, and stared at the ceiling. Joe sat next to her and put his hand on hers. "Are you okay?"

"I don't know. I'm making promises to Jenna that I don't know if I can keep."

"When you said we would figure this out, I'm sure she knew you meant we would do our best to figure this out. And we will do our best."

"What if our best isn't good enough?"

"It better be good enough, or all this worrying will be for nothing."

Katie turned her head and looked at Joe. She tried to suppress a laugh, but it came out like a snort. "I can always count on you to put things into perspective, Joe."

Joe smiled. "I will always be here to help."

Katie squeezed his hand. "Okay. Help think of what we should do next."

"Well, the police weren't able to get into the detective's phone. Maybe Billy from your old news station can help. You've been giving away business cards that say you are a freelance reporter. The last time you did a freelance news report, you were able to enlist Billy's help."

"That's right. Bob did say I could get Billy's help. He would only deduct his time from my pay."

"That's assuming he would want to do a story that is not related to Milwaukee."

"The station does more than just Milwaukee stories. I think he'll be interested."

"You should call and find out."

Katie picked up her phone and dialed a number. While it was ringing, she said, "I want to talk to Cheryl first."

"Hi, Katie," Cheryl said when she answered. "What's up?"

"Hi, Cheryl. Earlier, you mentioned that David's phone was locked, and you couldn't access it. Is that still the case?"

"That's right. Why do you ask?"

"I may know someone who can help with that. We need as much information as possible on David, including his full name, date of birth, address, phone number, email address, and the type of phone he has. Can you get that information for us?"

"Sure. I'm at the station now. Give me ten minutes."

Katie hung up and waited. It took a little longer than ten minutes, but Cheryl soon sent her a text with all the information she asked for. Katie then called her former boss, Bob Martin."

"It's good to hear from you again, Katie," Bob said after they exchanged greetings. "Ashley said your little boy turned one. Time sure does fly when you get old, although you probably haven't noticed that yet."

"Time flies when you're having fun, too, and we've been having a lot of fun."

"That's good to hear. So what do I owe the pleasure of this call?"

"I have a story for you, and we need Billy's help to uncover some information."

"What's your story, Katie?"

"Joe and I are here in my hometown because someone murdered the town's detective. The police charged my best friend's husband with the crime, but we are convinced they have the wrong guy. We then learned that someone murdered the mayor's daughter less than a day earlier, and the detective was investigating her murder when he was killed. We think they might be related because a piece of evidence from the crime scene went missing after the detective was murdered. It is also unusual for one murder to occur in this town, much less two so close together."

"It sounds like you got yourself a doozy of a case."

"We need your help to prove that my friend's husband is innocent. If you will let us ask Billy for his assistance, I will report what we find for no charge to the station."

"That sounds like a fair trade, Katie, but I can't legally allow you to work for free. We'll work something out. I'll transfer you over to Billy. I hope he can help you."

"Thanks so much, Bob."

"Hi, Miss Katie," Billy said when he answered the phone. He then added, "I mean, Katie. Mr. Martin said you need my help."

"We do," Katie said. "Someone murdered a police detective in my hometown, but his phone is locked. We think there may be some clues on that phone, but the police can't get into it."

Billy was silent for a few seconds before saying, "I can't help you get into his phone, but if he backed up his files to the cloud, I may be able to access those. I need you to send me as much information as you can on the man."

"I anticipated that," Katie said. "I'll email you everything I have. I appreciate your help. This is very important to me."

"I'll do what I can, but it may take a while."

"That's fine. Anything you can do is appreciated."

When Katie hung up, she asked Joe, "What do you want to do now?"

"There's not much we can do but wait. Let's take a walk. I want to go to the river and take some photographs."

"Okay, Honey, but there's not much around here worth photographing."

"There is beauty all around us. You only need to open your mind and see what is right in front of you."

"What are you, some kind of Zen master now?"

"No. I'm a photographer. I've been taking pictures for almost a hundred years. I have learned that beauty can be found in the ordinary. Sometimes you only need to frame it right."

"Okay, Joe. Get your camera. I want to see this beauty you are talking about."

They put their coats on, and Joe slung his camera over his shoulder. They walked towards the river. At the end of the road, a small hill led to railroad tracks that ran parallel to the Mississippi River. Beyond the tracks, trees and shrubs limited access to the river.

Joe held Katie's hand as they climbed the hill to the tracks. He stood on the tracks and looked both ways. He then removed his camera from his shoulder, knelt, and snapped a photo of the tracks and the surrounding area. "Look at this," he said as he held out the camera for Katie to see.

Katie knelt and looked through the viewfinder. "Oh, that's an interesting perspective."

Joe hit a couple of buttons, changing the camera's display to black-and-white. "What do you think now?" he asked.

Katie looked at the screen and said, "Oh, wow! You should print that. I bet that would look great in our living room."

"You see? There is beauty everywhere."

"You're right, Joe. I need to learn to be more observant."

They walked back to the road and continued north, holding hands. The temperature was a few degrees above freezing, but the air was still, so it didn't feel uncomfortably cold. After walking for two blocks, Katie asked, "Do you have a destination in mind, or are we just walking?"

"I remember there is a nature preserve north of town. I thought we could go there."

"That's at least another four blocks."

"Is that a problem for you?"

"No, of course not. I'm not that out-of-shape girl you met two years ago."

"When I first saw you, I thought your shape was great."

Katie playfully slapped Joe on the arm. "I'm not talking about that kind of shape."

The road along the river was lined with houses on the right, while the railroad tracks continued along its left. After passing the last house, they entered a thickly forested area. The road took a slight turn to the right. As they rounded the corner, Joe noticed a deer about fifty yards ahead.

"Look at that," he said.

"Very cool. What is that she's standing next to?"

"I don't know," he said as he raised his camera to his face. He extended the lens to its maximum magnification and saw that it was another deer.

He snapped a photo and said, "It's another deer. Perhaps a young one. I think it's hurt or sick."

Katie's smile faded as her expression turned to concern. "Oh, no! We've got to help it," she said as she walked quickly towards the deer.

"Slow down," Joe said as he attempted to catch up. "You'll scare them."

Katie slowed her pace. As they approached, Joe said, "It must be her fawn. The spots have faded, but you can tell it's young."

When they got to within fifty feet, the doe flicked her ears and stamped a hoof on the ground. She backed up and then stepped forward, letting out a loud snort.

Katie held out her hand as she inched forward. "It's okay," she said softly. "We just want to help."

The doe snorted again, but Katie slowly continued her progression forward, with Joe one step behind her. The mother deer, probably sensing they were there to help, gave up her protests, but remained vigilant.

The young deer had several gashes on her left hind leg and on her back. "It looks like a female," Joe said. "I think a predator attacked her. Maybe a coyote. The mother probably chased it away."

Katie put her hand on Joe's arm and said, "You need to heal her."

"What? I'm not an animal healer. I don't know anything about deer."

"You need to try, Joe. I'm so proud of what you've accomplished with your healing abilities these last two years, and I'm sure you are capable of more."

Joe hesitated and then said, "Okay, I'll try, but I can't promise anything."

He slowly approached the fawn, who grew nervous and tried to stand, but Joe gently placed a hand on her shoulder, which calmed her. "Here goes nothing," he said as he thought of the fawn as an extension of himself and connected with her.

There was no danger in the fawn telling anyone his secret, but Joe decided to block her from feeling what he felt anyway. He thought it might be a bit disconcerting for the animal.

Joe was amazed to be able to connect with another species. He felt everything that was happening inside the animal, but it was like visiting a foreign country for the first time without a map. Many things were familiar, but many more were significantly different from what he was used to. Fortunately, what he knew about how to stop bleeding and repair muscle damage was no different in this animal, so he set about doing that.

Ten minutes later, a pickup truck approached from the north. A middle-aged man with a scruffy beard, a heavy red flannel jacket, and a black knit hat buzzed down the window and asked, "Is everything alright? What happened to the deer?"

"A predator attacked her. Probably a coyote," Katie said.

"Do you need any help?"

"No, thanks. My husband is a vet."

The man looked at Joe and back at Katie. "Is his clinic nearby? I'd be happy to give you a ride there. You can put the deer in the back."

"Thanks for the offer, but I'm afraid the deer can't be moved yet."

"Okay," the man said. "Good luck to you."

A few minutes after the man drove away, Joe let go of the deer. "She still has some healing to do, but I think she will fully recover," he said.

The fawn slowly lifted her head. She seemed unsure what to do next. Finally, she drew her forelegs beneath her body and pushed upward. Her rear legs trembled as she struggled to stand. Joe crossed his fingers as the young deer attempted to gain her balance.

The mother deer took a cautious step forward. Her nostrils flared as she watched her little one find her footing. The doe's ears flicked, and she gave a soft, low grunt.

The fawn took a step toward her, then another. The mother held her ground like a human mother whose child is learning to walk. When her fawn closed the distance, she dipped her head and nuzzled the fawn's neck. The doe and fawn walked side by side to the forest's edge, slowed by the fawn's slight limp. When they reached the tree line, the doe briefly looked back at Katie and Joe, as if to say thank you. Soon they were gone, swallowed up by the forest.

Katie watched until they were out of sight, then put an arm around Joe's waist and said, "I knew you could do it."

"I wish I had thought to give you my camera," Joe said.

"Next time, Honey. Maybe we'll find an injured bear."

They continued walking until a clearing appeared on their left.

"This is what we saw on the map," Katie said.

"Joe took Katie's hand and said, "C'mon. Let's take a look."

It was a dirt road that led across the railroad tracks and to the river. When they reached the tracks, Joe said, "It's a clear path to the river's edge. If someone dumped a body in the river, I bet this is where they did it."

"No doubt," Katie said. "The only problem is there's no evidence anyone has been here."

"Yeah, that's unfortunate," Joe said. "I'm sure any tracks would be gone by now."

They walked to the river's edge, hoping to find a clue, but nothing presented itself, so they headed back to the house.

Chapter 10

Shortly before they returned to the house, Katie's phone beeped. She looked at it and then put it back in her pocket.

"What was that?" Joe asked.

"Billy sent us something."

"You don't want to look at it?"

"I do, but I want to read it on my laptop so you can see, too."

A minute later, they entered the house, removed their shoes and coats, and sat together on the sofa. Katie's laptop was on the end table, so she picked it up and checked her emails. She opened the one from Billy. "It's a link to David's cloud account," she said.

"What's a cloud account?"

Katie looked at Joe. His ignorance of technology still surprised her sometimes. "'The cloud refers to large computer systems that store backup files for people." She didn't know how to make the explanation any simpler.

Billy had given her the login information, so she signed on and looked at recent photos first. "There are a few photos from the day he died," Katie said. She opened the first photo.

"That's where we just were," Joe said as he looked at a photo taken from the street of the dirt road leading to the river.

"He must have had the same idea we had."

Katie advanced to the next photo. It was a close-up photo of a tire track.

"Well, what do you know? Someone did leave tracks," Joe said.

The next photo showed a tape measure stretched across the track. The photo after that showed the tape measure stretched across both tracks. The final image was a close-up of that measurement.

"I bet Billy could figure out what kind of vehicle these tracks came from," Katie said as she replied to the email with a message to Billy.

"Is there anything else in there?" Joe asked.

"I don't know. Let's see."

After a minute of searching, Katie said, "I found his search history."

"You mean there's a record of what he searched for?"

Katie looked at Joe, this time surprised that he understood something technical. "Yes," she said as she studied the screen. "There are several searches here. One is for 'High school class ring letter M.' Another is for 'Class ring designs M.' And then there's 'Colleges beginning with M.' I guess the Chief was wrong about it being a 'W.' Dave must have believed the ring was a college class ring, but was having trouble finding the right college."

"I wonder why he excluded high school class rings," Joe said. "Are there any high schools in this area that start with an 'M' besides Minaka?"

Katie thought for a moment and said, "No. Minaka would be the only one that I can think of."

"So, why would he exclude it?"

"I don't know. Maybe the type style was different."

"What I don't understand is why the school's name wasn't on the ring. Every class ring I ever saw had the school name on it."

"Perhaps he had it custom-made," Katie suggested. "Maybe he wanted to be different from the crowd, or he thought a simpler design was more appealing."

"So, if the ring was a simple letter, it could very well have been a 'W.'"

Katie shook her head. "I don't think so. Some type styles don't look right upside-down."

"Okay. Let's assume it's an 'M.' How do we know it's a school and not the first initial of the man's name?"

"Let's hope it's a school. If it's not, Mitch is in the hot seat again."

"Unfortunately, I don't think he ever left the hot seat," Joe said.

Katie closed her laptop and put it on the end table. She then picked up her phone and placed a video call to her mother. A few seconds later, her mom appeared on the screen. "Hi, Honey. How's your investigation going?"

"Slow, but we have a few leads. How is Joey doing?"

"He's doing wonderful. We're at the resort's restaurant now." She turned the phone to show Joey sitting in a highchair next to Karl. He had a fruit plate in front of him and put what looked like a sliced grape into his mouth. They heard Mary's voice say, "Joey, Mommy and Daddy want to say hi."

Joey looked to his right, and Mary said, "No. Over here." She shook the phone, causing the image to move quickly back and forth.

When Joey looked at the phone, Katie waved and said, "Hi, Joey."

Joey smiled briefly and then went back to eating grapes. Mary's face appeared again, and she said, "You see? He's doing fine."

Seeing her little boy pleased her greatly, and she wished they would solve the case quickly so they could go home. She sighed. "Thank you both so much for taking care of Joey."

"You don't have to thank us. It's our pleasure."

When Katie finished the call, she set the phone down, leaned back, and looked up at the ceiling.

Joe put his hand on hers and said, "Don't worry. We'll wrap this up and be home before you know it."

Katie sat up, looked at her watch, and said, "It's after four. We should talk to Emily before her office closes and tell her what we learned."

"We haven't learned anything about Mitch's case."

"No, but we learned something about Grace's case. I think she would want to know that. Then we can go out for dinner."

***

They got in Katie's car and drove to Emily Anderson's law office. Emily was with a client, so they waited until she was free. When they stepped into her office, Emily said, "Hi, Katie. Hi, Joe. Have a seat. Did you guys learn anything new?"

After they sat down, Katie said, "Yes and no. We didn't learn anything new about David Barclay's murder, but we did learn something about Grace Ellington's murder."

Emily tilted her head as a puzzled look appeared on her face. "Grace Ellington? Why are you looking into her murder?"

"We think the two murders might be connected," Katie said.

"Connected? How?"

"For several reasons. There hasn't been a murder in this town in years, and suddenly, there were two murders in less than a day. Furthermore, David was investigating Grace's murder when he was killed."

Emily leaned forward and shook her head. "I don't know. I admit that it's a bit of a coincidence, but it's not enough to draw any conclusions."

"David Barclay also found a ring on the victim with the letter 'M' carved into it. He believed that was the first letter of a college or university. That ring disappeared after he was murdered. Why would his killer take the ring if not to hamper the investigation into Grace's death?"

"Oh, wow!" Emily said. "You might be on to something."

121

"I think you should know there is a negative side to this," Joe said. Katie gave him a dirty look, but he continued. "Mitch has no alibi for when Grace was murdered, and, since we don't have the ring, there is no way to know if the 'M' was a school name or the name of a person."

Emily leaned back in her chair. "Mitch starts with an 'M.' That does complicate things. Have you spoken to Mitch about this?"

"We did," Katie said. "He said he worked late preparing for a case the next day. We also spoke with Jenna about it, and she told us that Mitch doesn't wear any jewelry except his wedding ring. We also found David's search history, which showed he was searching for colleges that started with the letter 'M.' We think he was convinced the ring represented a college."

"Did you learn anything else?"

Katie's phone beeped. She looked at it and saw a message from Billy. "Just a minute," she said. After viewing the message, she said, "As a matter of fact, I just got some new information. David took photos of tire tracks from an area where the killer most likely dumped the body into the river. My source informed me that those tracks belonged to a full-size pickup truck. He said it is most likely from either a Ford F-150 or a Dodge Ram 1500."

Emily was silent for a moment and said, "Mitch doesn't own a pickup truck, so that's good, but photos of tracks in a place that may or may not be relevant are not very helpful."

"We still have more work to do," Joe said, "but the detective thought they were relevant. We felt we should keep you in the loop."

Emily nodded. "Okay. I can see your reasoning for investigating the Grace Ellington murder. I think you should keep at it. If you can prove someone other than Mitch Hartney killed Grace Ellington, that might give us another suspect for David Barclay's murder."

After they said their goodbyes and stepped out of the law office, Katie said, "I don't think it was necessary to make Mitch look like the bad guy."

"I was merely pointing out what a prosecutor would point out. She needed to be ready for that."

Katie nodded slowly. "I guess you're right."

***

When they got in the car, Joe asked, "Where do you want to go for dinner?"

"Well, we have to leave town if we want to go anywhere fancy."

"Really? You don't have a nice restaurant in town?"

"You've been here before, Joe. When have we gone to a nice restaurant in town?"

"I don't know. I guess we haven't."

"It's a small town. The fanciest restaurant we have is the one where we had breakfast, and it's closed for dinner. Everything else is fast food or pizza."

"Hmm," Joe said.

Katie looked at Joe. His eyes were deep in thought. "What are you thinking about?" she asked.

"If you were a young man wanting to impress a woman on a first date, where would you take her?"

"Around here, there is only one place that I can think of."

Katie called to make a reservation, then drove south for twenty minutes before pulling into the parking lot of Ristorante al Fiume. The restaurant resembled an Italian villa, with cream-colored stucco, accented by arched windows trimmed in dark wood. A cobblestone path led from the parking area to the double wooden entry doors, softly lit by two wrought-iron lanterns. The restaurant's name was etched into the stucco above the door.

Inside, the atmosphere was warm and romantic. The foyer greeted patrons with polished marble flooring and a large saltwater aquarium to the left. Two clownfish darted in and out of a shell while a yellow, spotted pufferfish casually swam over them.

To the right was a coat-check. The man there offered to take Katie and Joe's coats, which they gladly relinquished to him.

"I haven't seen coat checks in ages," Joe said as they stepped towards the hostess.

"I told you this place was fancy."

The hostess, a middle-aged woman with her long, dark hair in a ponytail, was elegantly dressed in a black pantsuit paired with a white blouse. She smiled and said, "Buona sera. Welcome to Ristorante al Fiume. Do you have a reservation?"

"Yes. It's under 'Katie Novak,'" Katie said.

The woman looked down and said, "Oh, yes. I see you here." She picked up a couple of menus and said, "Follow me."

The main dining room was spacious but also intimate. Its tables stood far enough apart to offer some privacy. A white tablecloth covered each table. A candle and a single rose stood in the center. On the walls hung paintings of Italian villages.

When they reached their table, Katie showed the woman her phone. On it was a photo of Grace Ellington. "Did you, by chance, happen to see this woman here on Thursday evening?" she asked.

The woman looked at the photo and said, "Sorry. Thursday was my night off. Are you the police? Is the woman missing?"

"No. We are private investigators looking into her murder," Katie said.

"Oh, my. That's terrible. Perhaps Vince, your server, can help you. He'll be out shortly."

Less than a minute after the hostess left, a waiter showed up at the table. He was young, perhaps in his mid-twenties. He had medium-length dark hair that he slicked back using plenty of gel. He wore a crisp, white shirt, a black vest, and a black bow tie. "Welcome to Ristorante al Fiume," he said as he lit the candle on the table. "My name is Vince. I'll be your server tonight. Have you dined with us before?"

"I have, but he hasn't," Katie said.

The waiter looked at Joe and said, "Welcome. I will do my best to make sure you want to return. Can I start you two off with something to drink?"

"Yes, but we'd like to ask you a question first," Katie said.

"Sure. How can I help you?"

Katie showed the man the photo of Grace and asked, "Did you see this woman here last Thursday?"

The waiter looked at the photo and said, "Yes, I believe I did. She looks like someone I waited on that evening."

"Was she with a man?" Joe asked.

The waiter paused for a moment and said, "Yes, she was. What's this about?"

"Can you describe her date?" Katie asked.

"Are you guys cops or something?"

"We're private investigators," Katie said. "Can you describe the man?"

"Sure. He was tall, I think. I only saw him sitting. He had straight, dark-brown hair. He looked a little like you," he said, looking at Joe. "Did something happen to them?"

"Not them, her," Katie said. "She was killed that night."

A shocked look crossed the waiter's face. He put his hand over his heart and said, "Oh, my God! That's terrible. She seemed like such a sweet young woman."

"Do you have cameras here?" Joe asked.

"I'm afraid not. Our restaurant takes the privacy of our patrons very seriously."

"Okay. Thanks anyway," Joe said.

After the waiter took their drink order and left, Katie said, "The waiter described someone who doesn't look like Mitch. The woman at the coffee shop described someone similar. I think that's good evidence that Mitch is innocent."

"I think it casts doubt that he killed Grace, but it doesn't prove he is innocent of her murder, or the detective's murder. It's possible Grace's date didn't kill her. Maybe she surprised a burglar when she got home."

"Mitch is no burglar, Joe."

"I know. I'm simply pointing out other possibilities. Things Mitch's prosecutor will point out. I believe Mitch is innocent, but we need to prove it. So far, we are not close to doing that. Even if what we have is enough to keep him from being convicted and out of prison, which I don't think it is, there will always be doubt surrounding his involvement. You don't want him to live his life with people thinking he got away with murder. We need to erase all doubt."

"You're right as usual. We need to learn who this guy is."

"Yeah, but unfortunately, he is way too average. I bet there are a hundred men in this town that fit that description."

"Including you," Katie said.

"Yes. We need to find someone who looks like me."

Suddenly, there was a commotion at the table behind Katie, where an elderly couple sat. Joe couldn't see the man's face, but he saw concern on the woman's face and heard alarm in her voice. "Frank, are you okay? Frank! Frank!"

Joe stood and rushed over to the man, with Katie close behind. He grabbed the man's wrist, pretending to take his pulse, but instead connected to him. He could feel that a blood clot blocked an artery near the heart, and two other arteries were nearly blocked. Joe had become skillful in increasing the speed at which his blood clotted, which was useful whenever he was injured, but reversing a blood clot was something he had never encountered a need to do.

"He has a blood clot near his heart! Someone call 911!" Joe yelled. "Does anyone have aspirin?"

"How do you know that?" his wife asked.

An older man, several tables away, stood up. "I have some," he said as he approached. He took a small bottle out of his suit jacket and handed Joe an aspirin. "I have a bad heart. I keep these on me just in case."

"Thanks," Joe said as he took the aspirin from him. He handed it to the man and said, "Chew this before swallowing."

The man followed Joe's instructions while Joe worked on breaking up the blood clot. By the time the paramedics arrived, the pain had subsided, and the man was breathing normally again. His wife hugged him and then hugged Joe. "Thank you so much," she said.

Later, after an ambulance arrived and took the man away, Katie asked Joe, "Since when do you need drugs to heal someone?"

"Don't forget that I'm still learning. I've been healing myself for over a hundred years, but since learning how to heal others, I sometimes encounter issues I'm unfamiliar with."

"Yeah. I suppose you never had to deal with clogged arteries before."

"Exactly. I thought the aspirin would help while I figured out how to deal with the problem."

"Did you figure out a solution, or did the pills do all the work?"

"I did find a solution. It's hard to explain, but I learned long ago how to increase certain enzymes to help blood clot faster. With a little trial and error, I found something that worked to break those bonds. The downside is that when the man arrives at the hospital, the doctors will have trouble finding anything wrong with him. They'll probably tell him he had a severe case of heartburn."

Katie nodded. "Yeah, but he's still better off. Hopefully, he won't have the same problem in the future."

"Should we go to the hospital and tell him he needs to watch his diet?"

"Oh, yeah. I'm sure that will go over well," Katie said, "but maybe he needs to know."

"You told me before that I can't save everyone."

"Yes, I did. It feels different when you meet them, though."

Joe put his hand on Katie's but said nothing.

The waiter arrived at their table and said, "That was really something. I don't know what you did, but I'm happy that man was okay. The manager said that your meal is on the house tonight."

Chapter 11

Joe cooked breakfast the next morning. When they last shopped, he made sure they bought plenty of breakfast options, including the orange juice he likes to drink in the morning. He didn't mind going out for breakfast, but he preferred the comfort of home. Even though Katie's parents' house didn't technically count as home, it was close enough.

Joe put an omelet and fried potatoes on a plate and set it in front of Katie on the dining room table. He then cooked an omelet for himself and sat next to Katie.

"This is very good, Honey. Thanks for breakfast."

"It's my pleasure to serve you," Joe said, deciding it was a waste of time telling Katie that thanks were unnecessary.

"So, what should we do today?" Katie asked between bites.

"I was hoping you had an idea."

"I wish. The only real clue we have is that Grace was killed by someone driving a pickup truck who may or may not have gone to a college that starts with an 'M.' It seems every other adult in town owns a pickup truck, and there must be dozens of colleges that start with 'M.'"

"That does make it challenging," Joe said.

When they were done eating, Katie helped Joe clean the kitchen. After they finished washing the dishes and putting everything away, Katie's phone rang. She retrieved it from the dining room and looked at the screen. It was a local number she didn't recognize. She answered the call and put the phone to her ear. "Hello."

"Hello, Katie. This is Lisa from Minaka Perk. We spoke the other day about Grace Ellington."

"Oh, yes," Katie said. "Just a minute."

She put the phone on speaker as she walked back into the kitchen and stood next to Joe. "I'm here with my husband. What's going on?"

"I thought you would want to know that the man who was with Grace the other day returned this morning. He bought a coffee and a pastry and then left."

"How long ago was that?" Katie asked.

"Just now. About three or four minutes ago."

"Did you see what he was driving?" Joe asked.

"It was busy, so I only had time for a quick peek, but I saw he was driving a gray pickup truck. I couldn't tell the make."

"Which way did he go?" Joe asked.

"He was heading toward downtown," she said.

Joe raced out the door, not bothering to put on his shoes. He jumped the steps and ran down the sidewalk barefoot. When he reached the street, he looked left but saw nothing. When he looked right, he saw a gray pickup truck, but it was too far away to notice any detail. "Damn!" he said.

Katie stood by the door and called to Joe, "Did you see it?"

Joe shook his head and walked back to the house. When he stepped inside, he said, "I was ten seconds too late."

"That's okay," Katie said. "We know more now than we did two minutes ago."

"Hopefully, there aren't that many gray pickup trucks in this town."

Katie took out her phone and texted Billy. She asked for a list of everyone in Minaka who owned a gray Ford F-150 or a gray Dodge Ram 1500.

Joe watched her type the message into her phone and asked, "What if he doesn't live in town?"

Katie erased part of the message and asked for information on everyone in the county. "Is that good enough, or should I ask for the whole state?"

"No, I think that will work."

She sent the message and asked Joe, "What should we do while we wait for a reply?"

Joe put his arms around Katie and said, "I can only think of one thing."

Katie laughed. "How did I know you were going to say that?"

***

Two hours later, Katie heard her phone beep. She picked it up from the nightstand and looked at it. "It's a message from Billy."

"What does it say?"

"It's an Excel file. I need to look at it on my laptop," she said before getting dressed, retrieving her laptop from the living room, and placing it on the dining room table. Joe sat next to her while Katie opened the file and scrolled through it. "Wow! There are 440 names on this list."

"Seriously? That many people own gray full-size pickup trucks?"

"It would seem so."

"I guess we should have limited the search to only Minaka residents."

Katie rolled her eyes. "Which I started to do before you made me change it."

"I'm pretty sure I can't make you do anything."

"You're right. You can't. It's my fault for listening to you."

Joe shook his head. "I don't think it's a big deal. Can't we look only at the ones who live in town?"

"I might be able to sort the list." After some trial and error, she figured out how to sort the list by city and said. "We're down to 39 names."

"That's still a lot, but manageable. How many of those names are women?"

Katie scrolled through the list and said, "Five are women."

133

"Okay, so now we have 34 suspects. How many of those people do you know?"

Katie looked through the list and said, "Actually, many of the last names are familiar, but not the first names, except for one."

"I guess we should start by talking to people who are most familiar to you. Who should we question first?"

Katie smiled and nodded. "I know exactly where we should start."

They drove to Emily Anderson's office. Once inside, she invited them to sit down. "Have you learned anything new about the case?" she asked.

"Yes," Katie said. "We learned that Grace Ellington's killer most likely drives a gray, full-size pickup truck. We also learned your brother drives a gray, full-size pickup truck. To be exact, a gray 2021 Dodge Ram 1500, a model that matches the tire tracks Detective Barclay had found."

A look of shock came over Emily's face. "Wait a minute. Are you saying you think Jimmy killed Grace Ellington?"

"No, not at all," Joe said. "Katie is only pointing out that he is one of several possibilities."

"Exactly how many 'possibilities' are there?" Emily asked, stressing the word "possibilities."

Joe looked at Katie, who shrugged. He looked back at Emily. "Thirty-four."

"Thirty-four? Are you kidding me? You can't come here and accuse my brother of murder with thirty-three other suspects." She looked at Katie.

"Are you sure you are not singling out my brother because of the history you two have together?"

"I think you misunderstand our intentions," Katie said. "We came here simply to inform you that he is on our suspect list and also to ask you where he works these days so we can talk to him about it. We plan on looking at everyone."

Emily stared at Katie for several seconds before saying, "He works in the maintenance department at the Rivercrest Hotel in La Crosse."

"Do you know if he's working today?"

"I have no idea. I don't keep tabs on my brother."

"Okay, thank you, Emily. We'll keep you posted." Katie said before she and Joe left the office.

"That could have gone better," Joe said when they got outside.

"Yeah. I guess I didn't consider how strong family ties can be."

"Is she right? Are we focusing on him because of your resentment for him?"

Katie feigned shock. "What? Do you think I would be so petty? What happened between us happened fifteen years ago."

"Yes, but you formed a negative opinion of him then, and nothing has changed since to cause you to alter that opinion."

They reached the car and climbed in. Katie closed her door, put her seatbelt on, and looked at Joe. "You sure do have a way with words sometimes. Let's check out his house first, just in case today is his day off."

Joe looked surprised. "You know where he lives?"

"Relax, Joe. I don't keep tabs on him. His address was in the list Billy sent us."

His house was less than a half mile from downtown. It was a single-story midwestern ranch-style home with an attached one-car garage on the left. The driveway was empty. The truck could have been in the garage. They couldn't be sure.

Katie parked on the street, and they walked to the small wooden porch. When Katie rang the doorbell, Joe wondered whether he would need to step down to make room for the door if it opened. He needn't have been concerned. The door didn't open.

Katie looked at Joe and said, "It looks like we're going to La Crosse."

It took about half an hour to drive to the hotel where Jimmy worked. It was a modern hotel that stood five stories high and overlooked the Mississippi River. Katie parked the car, and they went inside.

At two stories high, the lobby was impressive. What looked like a huge glass windchime hung from the ceiling. To the left was a counter with two employees behind it, helping guests. To the right were several sofas and chairs, along with a few tables in the center of the area. There were no people in that area, but several were at the front desk.

Katie and Joe waited for their turn, then told the woman behind the counter they were there to see Jimmy Anderson.

"Can I ask your names?" she asked.

"Just tell him Katie needs to talk to him."

The woman nodded and picked up her phone. She dialed a number and waited. After a few seconds, she said, "There is someone in the lobby named Katie who wants to speak with you." When she hung up, she said, "He'll be down in a few minutes."

They moved aside so the woman could help the next guest, but waited nearby. Three minutes later, Jimmy Anderson appeared. He was almost as tall as Joe, about five-eleven, and had the same straight, dark hair. He was clean-shaven, wore dark gray pants, a black belt, and a gray short-sleeve shirt. His name badge said, "J. Anderson."

"Katie," he said when he approached. "I heard you were in town." He hugged her and asked, "What brings you here?"

Katie put her hand on Joe's arm and said, "Jimmy, this is my husband, Joe."

"Oh, uh, hi," he said and shook Joe's hand. He looked back at Katie. "Why did you drive all the way out here to see me?"

Katie pointed at one of the tables and said, "Let's talk over there."

They all sat at a table, and Jimmy asked, "Okay, what's this about?"

"We're investigating the death of Grace Ellington," Katie said.

"The mayor's daughter? Really? I heard you quit that news station."

"I did, but I still do freelance work for them."

"Interesting," Jimmy said. "So, you think your old station will buy this story?"

"Well, yes, but we came to town to prove Mitch Hartney didn't kill David Barclay. Your sister officially hired us, although it's pro bono."

"That's great that you want to help Mitch, and I wish you luck, but what does that have to do with Grace Ellington, or me, for that matter?"

"We think the two murders are connected. We think the person who killed Grace also killed David Barclay," Katie said.

"From what I heard, the police have a strong case against Mitch. If you are right, that probably means Mitch killed Grace, too."

"No. We have evidence to suggest someone else did it."

Jimmy looked surprised at the revelation. "Evidence? What evidence do you have?"

Joe, attempting to speed up the conversation, said, "We are fairly certain Grace's killer drove a gray, full-size pickup truck, like the one you own."

A look of shock crossed Jimmy's face. "Wait a minute. Are you accusing me of Grace's murder?"

"No, no. We're not accusing you of anything," Katie said.

"Did you kill her?" Joe asked bluntly.

The shocked look again crossed Jimmy's face. "No! Of course not!" He looked at Katie. "You know I wouldn't do anything like that."

Katie looked at Joe, annoyed, and then back at Jimmy. "We simply want to cross you off our suspect list."

"Where were you Thursday evening?" Joe asked.

"Thursday? Uh, I worked until six and went home."

"Did you stay home all evening?" Katie asked.

"Yeah. I had to work the next morning."

"Can you prove it?" Joe asked.

"Yes, I can, but I shouldn't have to. You're not the police." He stood up and turned to Katie. "It was nice seeing you again, Katie, but I have work to do. This conversation is over."

When he walked away, Katie slapped Joe on the arm and said, "What is wrong with you? Don't you know you can catch more flies with honey than with vinegar?"

"The honey wasn't working. Did you see the look of surprise on his face when we told him the killer drove a truck like his? Either he was surprised that the killer drove a similar truck, or he was surprised that we learned that information. In either case, he would not have told us anything if we used honey. We needed to shock him into revealing something that he didn't want to reveal."

"Either way, it didn't work. So how do we find out if he's telling the truth or not?"

"I have an idea about that," Joe said as he stood and motioned for Katie to follow him.

When they got outside, Katie asked, "What is your idea?"

Joe scanned the parking lot and said, "We need to find where his truck is parked."

"Oh, that's a great idea," Katie said.

They walked around the parking lot and eventually found the gray pickup truck parked in an area behind the hotel. "Take a picture of the tires," Joe said.

Katie took out her phone and snapped a couple of photos of one of the tires, ensuring she got the tread pattern.

When they returned to the car, Joe asked, "Do his tires match?"

Katie looked at the photos Detective Barclay had taken of the tracks and compared them to the ones she had just taken. She switched back and forth between the photos a couple of times and said, "They're different. The pattern doesn't match."

"Well, now we know we can scratch your ex-boyfriend off our list."

"You know, it's weird. When I saw Jimmy's name on the list, I almost wanted it to be him, but now I feel relieved."

"That's a good thing. It means you've matured."

"Are you suggesting I was immature?"

"In some ways, everyone is immature. It takes years to gain the wisdom to recognize when immature thoughts creep into your mind. In your case, you probably thought Jimmy didn't suffer enough for what he did to you, but then realized that his suffering has nothing to do with your happiness."

"You're a wise man, Joe. You may be right. I don't know. I know when we were talking to him, I imagined him going to prison and realized I didn't want him to suffer that much."

"If we find the killer, or killers, someone will go to prison."

"Yeah, I know. I don't wish that on anyone. I would prefer that people were kind to other people and didn't kill them."

Joe nodded. "That would be nice, but if the world were perfect, what would we investigate? You'd be bored."

Katie looked at Joe. "You're right. Now I feel like a bad person."

"No. You are not a bad person. You are the opposite of a bad person. We live in an imperfect world, and you are passionate about getting justice for people who were wronged."

"I suppose," Katie said. "Let's talk about something else. Do you want to get something to eat before we head back to town?"

"Yes. I'm hungry. Do you know of a good restaurant in this area?"

Katie started the car and looked at Joe. "Of course I do. You should know me by now."

Chapter 12

Katie drove for less than two blocks and parked on the street across from an old, four-story brick building. The top three floors were condos or apartments, but the entire ground floor was a restaurant called "The Captain's Table."

Joe looked at the name and said, "This is a good choice. We haven't had seafood in a while."

They got out of the car and walked across the street. "It's not only seafood," Katie said. "They have great steaks, too, and you can even get vegetarian dishes. I know how you like your healthy food."

"You say that like it's a bad thing. Healthy food can be delicious."

"You will never convince me that a salad can taste better than a well-cooked filet."

"I wouldn't try. I love a good filet, but you have to have a variety."

They stepped inside, where a woman greeted them and asked how many were in their party.

"Just two of us," Katie said.

"Just a moment," she said and stepped away.

"I think everyone knows we need a variety in our diets," Katie said. "That's why most restaurants serve salads with the meal."

"That is a tradition that started back in the forties after the war. When I was young, I don't recall ever getting a salad at a restaurant. Of course, going to a restaurant back then was not as common as it is today."

The woman returned, picked up a couple of menus, and said, "Follow me, please."

The restaurant was not busy at lunchtime, so they were able to get a table near one of the large windows that overlooked the river. The tables were similar to those at the Italian restaurant they had gone to for dinner, with white linen tablecloths and a candle in the center. The woman put their menus on the table and said, "Your server will be with you shortly."

The chairs had thick, leather cushions. When Joe sat down, he said, "This is nice. Most restaurants have uncomfortable chairs."

"That's because they don't want people to hang out after their meal is over," Katie said.

"That is true unless most of their profit comes from alcohol. Then they want you to stay all night."

Their server came and took their orders. When he left, Joe asked, "Who's the next person on the list that you want to check out?"

Katie took out her phone and opened the list Billy sent her. She looked through the names and said, "I don't know. As I mentioned earlier, I recognize many of the last names on the list, but not the first names. I'm afraid I don't know any of these other people."

143

"Really? You grew up here."

"I left when I was eighteen. Things have changed since then. People have changed since then."

"Yeah, I see your point. What about the last names you know?"

Katie looked through her list. "Well, there's George Ellington. That's the Mayor's last name. I remember he had a brother who lived in town. This could be him, or he could be his brother's son. He could also be someone unrelated."

She continued looking. "Here's someone named Kyle Bronson. That's the chief's last name. I have no idea whether this person is related or not. Then there's Charles White. I went to school with a pair of twins named Rose and Mary White."

"Rosemary?"

"Yeah. I'm sure that their parents thought they were being creative. Anyway, they had a younger brother, but I don't remember his name. This person could be him, or he could be his father, or he could be someone else."

"I guess it doesn't matter if you know them or not," Joe said. "Are their ages or dates of birth on the list?"

"I wish," Katie said. "That would be helpful."

"That list turned out to be bigger than I expected. Maybe you can ask Billy to narrow it down to males who live in town and are under forty."

"I think that's a good idea, Joe, but if Grace liked older men, we might miss someone."

"I think it's worth the risk. Besides, the woman at the coffee shop said he was young."

"She also said everyone looked young to her."

"We have to start somewhere."

Katie typed a message to Billy and then said, "Hopefully, he can get that information soon."

***

After lunch, they drove back to Katie's parents' house. A few minutes after they arrived, Katie got a notification from Billy. She brought her laptop to the dining room and sat at the table. Joe sat next to her as she opened the email from Billy. "It's a revised list," she said.

"How many names are left?"

Katie counted the names. "Eighteen."

"That's better than thirty-four but still too many. How old was Grace Ellington?"

"I'm not sure. I think she was around twenty-four."

"Didn't the woman at the bank say the guy she met was someone she used to know?"

"Yeah, but we don't know where Grace knew him from."

"Think about it," Joe said. "When people mention that they used to know someone, that usually means years have passed since they last saw them. At twenty-four years old, that means she was probably in college or high school when she last saw this person. There's a good chance that she met this person in school. If that were the case, I would bet he is within about three years of her age and probably closer to one year."

Katie nodded. "That makes sense."

"Look at that list again and include only people born between 1998 and 2004."

Katie looked through the list again. "Let's see. There's Michael Reese, Jeremy Carter, Kyle Bronson, and Charles White."

"Okay. Four we can deal with. Let's drive by each of their houses and see if their trucks are there."

Katie nodded and drove toward Michael Reese's house. She didn't need to use her GPS, as she was familiar with most of the roads in town. However, once she reached the correct road, she did need to check the house numbers to ensure she was traveling in the right direction.

Michael Reese's house was a split-level home, similar to Katie's parents' house but without the garage. A gray Ford F-150 was parked in the driveway behind a white Honda Civic.

Katie parked on the street behind the driveway and brought up the photo of the tire tracks on her phone before she and Joe got out of the car. She squatted down near one of the truck's rear tires and compared the photo to the tire. After looking at the tire and then her phone several times, she said. "It's a match. This tire has the same tread pattern."

"Are you sure?" Joe asked.

She handed her phone to Joe and said, "Have a look."

146

Joe checked the image against the tire's tread pattern and said, "You're right. It matches."

"Let's go talk to him," Katie said, starting to walk toward the house, but Joe held her back.

"Wait. It could be dangerous. You stay behind me."

"Joe, I appreciate that you want to protect me, but we're just going to ask a few questions. Nothing is going to happen."

"Even so, I'd feel better if you stood behind me."

"Okay, fine. Lead the way."

Joe knocked on the door, and they waited. After about thirty seconds, the door opened several inches, and a young woman looked out through the opening. She looked to be in her early twenties with long, unkempt blond hair. "Can I help you?" she asked.

Katie stepped forward and said, "Hi. I'm Katie, and this is my husband, Joe. We are looking for Michael. Is he here?"

The sound of a baby crying interrupted them. The young woman said, "Just a minute and went back inside the house, leaving the door partially open. She returned, holding a baby boy about Joey's age. He quickly quieted as his mom gently rocked him.

"We have a little boy at home," Katie said. "He just turned one."

"Oh, so you know what it's like. Mikey will be one in three weeks," she said, looking down at the boy who had now fallen asleep. He can get cranky when he's tired."

"We know all about that," Katie said.

147

"Can we speak with Michael?" Joe asked.

"I'm sorry, but he's asleep. He works third shift at the plant."

"You mean the paper mill?" Katie asked.

"Is there another plant around here?"

"Not that I know of."

"What time does he work?" Joe asked.

"He starts at midnight. Why? What's this all about?"

"We're investigating the death of Grace Ellington," Katie said.

"The mayor's daughter? What happened to her was terrible. I knew her personally, but what does Mike have to do with it?"

Do you mind if we come in?" Katie asked.

"Well, I guess it will be all right." She stepped aside and let Katie and Joe come in. She led them to the living room. It was surprisingly clean for a home with a one-year-old boy living in it. "Would you like to have a seat?"

"No, thank you," Joe said. We'll only be a couple of minutes. Was Mike home the night Grace Ellington died?" Joe asked. "It would have been around nine in the evening."

"What are you asking? Do you think my husband had something to do with her death?"

"No. We don't have any suspects at this time," Katie said. "We're just following up on a lead."

"What lead brought you here?"

Katie looked at Joe and then back at the woman. "Well, we have evidence to suggest the killer drove a gray pickup truck with a tire pattern that matches the pattern on your husband's truck."

A look of shock came over the woman's face. "What? No! Mike had nothing to do with her death. He has been home every evening with me."

Joe had been looking around the room and noticed a wedding photo hanging on the wall. The woman was in the photo wearing a white wedding gown. Her husband stood next to her, wearing a black tuxedo. He had medium-length blond hair and was slightly taller than the woman, who was of average height. "I assume this is Michael," Joe said.

"That's right," the woman said.

"Look at this, Katie," Joe said, pointing at the photo.

Katie stepped closer to the photo and examined it closely. She then said, "Thank you for your time, Mrs. Reese. We're sorry to bother you."

The woman looked at the photo, a confused expression on her face. "That's it? Do you believe what I told you?"

"We believe you," Katie said. "Your husband doesn't match the description of the man we are looking for. I don't suppose he lent his truck out to anyone last Thursday?"

"No. Nobody drives that truck except Mike."

"Okay. Thanks again for your time," Katie said.

When they returned to the car, Katie said, "I thought we had our guy. What are the odds that the truck and the tires match but not the guy?"

"Maybe that is the standard tire for that truck, or maybe that is what the local tire shop carries as a replacement."

"I suppose that makes sense. It would be easier if tires were like fingerprints."

"At least we were able to eliminate someone. It's a start. Who's next on the list?"

Katie checked her phone. "Jeremy Carter is next."

They drove to Jeremy Carter's house, which was just a couple of blocks away. It was an older single-story home with a driveway to the left that led to a one-car detached garage behind the house. There were no vehicles in the driveway, but the pickup truck might have been in the garage. Katie and Joe stepped onto the large wooden porch. Katie rang the doorbell, and they waited. After a minute, Katie rang the bell again. Joe looked through the window but saw no one.

"He must be at work," he said. "We can try again later."

When they returned to the car, Katie looked at her phone and said, "Kyle Bronson is next."

"He's probably at work, too," Joe said. "Let's go back to the house. I'll cook a nice dinner, and then we can check on him afterwards. If he works a normal job, he should be home by then."

When they returned to the house, Joe gathered the necessary ingredients and took a large frying pan out of the cabinet. He put the pan on the stove and added a small amount of oil. He then cut chicken breasts into chunks and added them to the pan.

Katie sat at the counter and watched him work. "What are you cooking, Honey?"

"It's a chicken stir fry."

"Ah, you decided to do Chinese tonight."

"It's similar, but this is actually a Japanese version."

"What's different about it?"

"A few things, but mainly it has a teriyaki flavor. I think you'll like it."

"I'm sure I will. I like everything you make."

"You didn't like those lentils I made for you last month. You said they were disgusting."

"Yeah, but that wasn't your fault. Nobody can make lentils taste good."

"It's too bad you don't like them because they're good for you."

"You're good for me. I don't need no stinkin' lentils."

Joe laughed. "I guess we can do without those stinkin' lentils."

"I feel like we are getting close to finding Grace's killer. Once we do, we should be able to tie him to David's killer and free Mitch."

"I hope you're right, Katie, but you know the old saying about counting your eggs before they're hatched."

"I know, but we're not counting eggs here. I really believe we will know the killer by tomorrow."

"As I said, I hope you're right."

After dinner, they drove to Kyle Bronson's home. He lived near the edge of town, on a street that contained several quadplexes. Katie pulled in front of Kyle's quadplex. His truck was parked in the far right parking spot. Katie parked behind the truck. The sun had gone down, but there was still enough light to see the tread pattern on the truck's tires. Katie compared it to the photo on her phone and said, "We have another match."

"Okay, let's talk to him, but stand behind me, just in case."

"Don't be ridiculous, Joe," Katie said as she pushed past him.

Kyle lived in unit D on the right. There was no doorbell, so Katie knocked on the door. A few moments later, the door opened, and a young man appeared. It was the same young man they saw at the police station talking to the chief."

"Can I help you?" he asked.

Katie looked at Joe with a surprised expression on her face. She looked back at the man and said, "We saw you at the police station. You're the chief's son."

"That's right. What is this about?"

"We'd like to know where you were on Thursday evening," Joe said.

Kyle furrowed his eyebrows, his gaze darting from Joe to Katie and back. "What? Who are you?"

"My name is Katie Novak, and this is my husband Joe. We are private investigators working for Mitchell Hartney's attorney."

"Who's Mitchell Hartney?"

"He's the man whom the police think killed Detective Barclay," Katie said.

"Oh, that asshole. He should get the chair for what he did."

"Wisconsin doesn't have capital punishment," Joe said.

"That's too bad."

"We're not here to talk about Detective Barclay. We're here to find out where you were when Grace Ellington was killed."

"Grace? You think I killed Grace?"

"We don't know," Joe said. "Did you?"

"Of course not. Why would I kill Grace?"

"You tell me," Joe said.

"You have a lot of nerve coming here and accusing me of murder. You know who my father is, so you must know you are walking on dangerous ground here."

"We are not accusing you of anything," Katie said. "We are talking to everyone on our suspect list. We simply want to know where you were on Thursday evening."

After a short pause, Kyle said, "I was home that night."

"Can you prove that?" Joe asked.

"No, I can't prove it. I was here alone. I shouldn't have to prove it. I'm no killer. I think you need to leave now."

"One more question," Katie said.

"No! No more questions," he said before closing the door.

"Well, that could have gone better," Joe said.

"That's a common theme lately."

Joe looked back at Kyle's apartment and said, "An innocent man doesn't behave like that. Can you ask Billy if he can dig up information on that guy?"

After they both got into the car, Katie typed a message to Billy. She started the engine and said, "Billy's off work now, so we won't know anything until tomorrow. Let's go back to the house. I want to investigate this guy a little myself."

"He may be right, Katie. We could be getting into dangerous territory."

"Are you afraid of the chief?"

"No, but he could impede our investigation."

"So, should we quit investigating, so our investigation won't get impeded?"

"When you say it like that, it makes my comment sound stupid."

"I'm going to take a page out of your book and not sugarcoat it. You are the smartest man I know, but your comment was stupid."

"I was merely pointing out that we should be careful."

"Okay. We'll be careful."

When they returned to the house, Katie put her laptop on the table and opened it. Joe sat next to her and asked, "What are you looking for?"

"I don't know exactly. I'm looking through Kyle Bronson's Facebook page. I want to get a sense of who the man is."

After a few minutes, Joe retrieved the book he had packed and continued reading it. About ten minutes later, Katie said, "I think I found something."

Joe put his book down and looked at the screen. "What did you find?"

"I had to go back pretty far through Kyle's Facebook posts, but look at what I found."

Joe saw a photo of Kyle with Grace Ellington. They had their arms around each other. "Were they a couple?" he asked.

"Yes. It looks like they were together at the end of their senior year of high school. I don't know what happened to them after that, but she disappeared from his posts."

"So, they ran into each other at the coffee shop and decided to make another go at it."

"It would seem so."

"We need to go to that coffee shop tomorrow and show his photo to that barista. If she identifies him, we will have our man."

"I told you we were getting close," Katie said.

Chapter 13

Joe made breakfast again the next morning. As they were preparing to leave, Katie's phone rang. She looked at it and saw it was Cheryl. She answered it and said, "Good morning, Cheryl."

"Good morning, Katie. I don't know what you did yesterday, but the chief is pissed. He wants to see you right away."

"We don't work for him. He can't make us do anything."

"He said if you are not in his office in thirty minutes, he will have me arrest you for harassment and obstruction of justice. What did you do to make him so angry?"

"Well, we might have questioned his son about Grace's murder."

"Oh, my God. That would do it. I suggest you come in. I really don't want to arrest you."

"Okay, Cheryl. We'll be there shortly."

Katie hung up and looked at Joe. "That dangerous ground you were talking about. We're on it."

They arrived at the police station twenty minutes later. Cheryl was there and escorted them into the chief's office. She stepped out and closed the door. "What the hell were you two doing harassing my son about the Grace Ellington case?" The chief yelled. He took a deep breath and composed himself before saying in a calmer voice, "You told me you were investigating Dave's murder. I agreed to help you with that, but you are way overstepping here."

"I'm sorry, Chief, but we weren't harassing your son," Katie said. "We just asked him a few questions. We think the two killings are related and the same person committed both murders."

"I think you're grasping at straws, but if that's true, then your client is guilty of two murders, in which case, you should leave my son out of it."

"We are convinced someone else killed Grace Ellington and then killed David Barclay to cover up the crime," Katie said.

"Really? Who exactly do you think this person is?" the chief asked.

"We have information that points to your son, Kyle," Joe said.

"Kyle? That's ridiculous. Kyle wouldn't hurt a fly. You're so desperate to get your friend off the hook that you are willing to hurt other people in the process. I won't let you do it. If you bother my son again, I'll have you arrested."

"But Chief, we…" Katie started to say.

Joe put his hand on Katie's arm and shook his head. He looked at the chief and said, "We promise not to bother your son again without sufficient evidence."

"Get out of my sight," the chief said, waving them out the door.

"How did it go?" Cheryl asked when they got to the lobby.

"He didn't arrest us, so it could have been worse," Katie said.

"I would try to stay under the radar for a while if I were you."

Katie shook her head. "That's not gonna happen."

When they got outside, Katie asked Joe, "Why did you stop me in there?"

"Two reasons. First, if Kyle is guilty, his father will want to protect him, so it's better we keep him in the dark about what we know. Second, if Kyle is innocent, it would be best not to accuse him of a crime in front of his father."

"That makes sense, but you already accused his son of the crime."

"I shouldn't have done that, and I didn't want you to double down on my mistake."

"Forget about the chief. Let's go to the coffee shop and put this case behind us."

***

The woman at the coffee shop who had seen the man Grace talked to the morning of her death was busy, so Katie and Joe waited in line. While they waited, Katie found Kyle's Facebook profile photo on her phone. When the woman was free, she showed her the photo and asked if that was the man she had seen that morning.

"That's him. How did you find him?"

"Your tip about the gray truck helped," Joe said.

"Did that man kill that sweet young girl?"

"We think so," Katie said, "but now we have to prove it."

"If he did kill her, I hope he gets put away for a very long time."

"As do we," Katie said.

When they returned to the car, Katie's phone beeped. She saw it was a message from Billy. She opened it and read silently. After a while, Joe asked, "Well, what does it say?"

"It's information on Kyle. Most of it is unimportant, but this is interesting. It says he is married. He married someone named Jane Murphy just over a year ago. She filed for divorce in late November, citing physical and verbal abuse."

"That didn't last long. It sounds like the guy has a temper."

"Yeah. I think we need to confront him."

"If he does have a temper, it could be dangerous," Joe said. "Maybe we should get Cheryl involved."

"No. We can't ask Cheryl to risk her job. She would surely get fired if she were to question the chief's son."

"I'm sure he could make our life miserable, too."

"We have to do something, Joe. We can't let Mitch rot in jail."

"Okay, we'll talk to him at his job. He probably won't cause trouble there. Just in case, I'll talk to him. You can stand behind me in case there's trouble."

"I'm not gonna do that. Men who hit their wives are insecure. He would never hit me with another man around."

"I thought I wouldn't have to worry about you on this case, but I was wrong."

"Relax, Joe, we'll be fine."

"Is there anything else in there that might help us?"

"Yes," Katie said. "It says he graduated from the University of Minnesota."

"Oh, that would explain the ring with the letter 'M.'"

"Exactly," Katie said.

They drove to the paper mill, which was about five miles south of town. As they followed the road along the river, the mill came into view. The complex was massive. Several buildings connected by pipes and conveyor belts occupied much of the land. Mountains of logs and wood chips waited in the spaces between the buildings. Three tall smokestacks pushed white steam into the air. An endless stream of trucks rumbled in and out, adding to the mountain of logs, while cranes and tractors removed the wood as quickly as the trucks added to the piles.

A sharp, sulfurous smell, almost like rotten eggs, permeated the air inside the car as they approached the gate. Katie wrinkled her nose and said, "I don't know how these workers handle the smell."

"I'm sure if you worked here, you wouldn't notice it after a couple of days."

"I would not want to test that theory."

Katie rolled her window down when she reached the gate. She told the guard they were there to speak to Kyle Bronson. He directed them to the administration building. Katie had to struggle to hear him over the loud hum of machinery.

She followed his instructions and parked in a lot labeled "Visitor Parking." The administration building stood in contrast to the rest of the facility. Instead of a cold, steel building, the two-story brick structure looked more like a small-town city hall.

Joe opened one of the double glass doors, held it for Katie, then followed her inside. The inside looked far less charming than the building's exterior. The floor was white linoleum. The walls were painted an eggshell white. Several doors lined the perimeter of the lobby. All were closed, and none had windows. There was a window on each side of the entrance with several plastic chairs under each window. Straight ahead, a woman sat behind a desk. It looked very similar to the police station's waiting room, only bigger.

Katie and Joe stepped up to the desk.

"Can I help you?" the woman asked.

"Yes," Katie said. "We are here to see Kyle Bronson. It's important."

"Can I get your names?"

"Katie and Joe Novak," Katie said.

The woman picked up her phone and dialed a number. After a few seconds, she said, "There's a Katie and Joe Novak here to see you." After a short pause, she said, "I don't know. They said it's important."

She hung up the phone and said, "He'll be out shortly."

A minute later, the door to the far right opened, and Kyle Bronson stepped into the lobby. He wore a white polo shirt with the company logo, navy blue pants, and brown work boots. The annoyance on his face was obvious. He led them toward the door, away from the receptionist, and whispered, "What are you doing here? Didn't my father tell you to stop harassing me?"

"We're not harassing you," Katie said loud enough for the receptionist to hear. "We just need to clear up a few things."

"We can talk here or outside," Joe said.

"Fine," Kyle said. He pushed the door open and stepped out into the cold without a coat, followed closely by Katie and Joe. He crossed his arms over his chest, holding the opposite arms, trying to keep the heat from escaping his body. The temperature had dropped to below freezing, and each breath hung in the air like steam from a locomotive. They stopped walking when they reached the parking lot.

"Let's cut to the chase," Katie said. "We have evidence that points to you in the death of Grace Ellington."

"You're crazy. I didn't kill anyone, and I don't think you have any evidence. I think you are trying to intimidate me into confessing to something I didn't do."

"Really?" Katie asked. "You didn't take Grace on a date Thursday evening?

Kyle froze. He had a look of shock on his face.

"After dinner, you didn't bring her home and then slap her, causing her to fall and split her head open on the concrete?"

Katie stepped closer. "Then you didn't put her dead body in your truck, drive to a secluded spot north of town, and dump her in the river like a piece of trash?"

Kyle opened his mouth, but nothing came out. He composed himself and said, "I don't know what you are talking about. I went straight home after work that day and didn't leave until the next morning."

"Can you prove that?" Joe asked.

"No. I can't prove it. I live alone."

"You have plenty of neighbors," Joe said. "Should we ask them if your truck was parked there all night?"

This time, the shock on his face turned to panic. "Go ahead. Ask them."

"We spoke to one of Grace's coworkers," Katie said. "Grace told her she had a date with someone she used to know that evening. She told her that she had run into him at the coffee shop where she gets her morning coffee. We showed your photo to the woman at the coffee shop, and she confirmed the man she met was you."

"We also learned you dated Grace in high school," Joe added, "and you were abusive to your wife, which means you have an anger management problem."

Kyle's mouth hung open, but again, nothing came out.

"You took her to Ristorante al Fiume that night," Katie said. "A waiter confirmed she was there with someone who matches your description. I'm sure when we go back there and show him your photo, he will identify you. And what happened to your ring? You know, the one with the letter 'M.' The one you had made when you went to the University of Minnesota."

"I don't have a ring like that."

"Not now, but you did. We have a photo of you wearing it." Katie lied.

Kyle took a deep breath and raised his hands. "Okay! Okay! You got me. It was an accident. She fell and hit her head. I feel terrible about it, but I didn't murder her."

"You slapped her hard enough to knock her down," Katie said.

"She hit me first," Kyle said defensively. "It was a knee-jerk reaction."

"Why did she hit you?" Joe asked.

"There. You see? That's why I didn't tell anyone. If a woman hits a man, it's perfectly okay, but if a man hits a woman, he's a criminal."

"If a man has a habit of hitting a woman, he has a problem," Joe said. "That's why your wife filed for divorce."

"You don't know everything," Kyle said. "She was the violent one, but since she's a woman, everyone thinks she's the victim."

"You killed Detective Barclay to cover up what you did," Katie said. "You can't blame gender bias for something like that."

"Wait! What? You think I killed the detective. That's absurd. I didn't do that."

"Do you expect us to believe that?" Joe asked. "Where were you when the detective was murdered?"

"I was working."

"You were here?" Joe asked.

"Well, technically, I was in town around that time. I was at the hardware store picking up some parts. Ask them."

"The hardware store is two blocks from the police station," Katie said. You could have easily made a detour."

"No! I didn't! I wouldn't!"

Katie looked at Joe. "Why don't you do that lie detector thing on him?"

"What lie detector thing?"

"You know? That thing you did to me the other day."

"That works on you because I know you."

"That shouldn't matter. I bet it will work on him, too."

Kyle looked confused. "What are you guys talking about?"

"Joe has a special talent. He can tell if someone is lying simply by feeling their pulse."

"Really? Is that possible?"

"If you are willing, we can find out together," Joe said.

Kyle hesitated and then said, "Fine. What do I have to do?"

"Hold out your wrist," Joe said.

Kyle held up his left hand and said, "Whatever you're gonna do, do it fast. It's cold out here."

Joe held his wrist with his right hand and connected to him. He could feel everything that was happening inside Kyle's body, but he blocked Kyle from feeling what he felt. "What is your name?" Joe asked.

"Kyle Bronson."

"What did you do to cause Grace Ellington to hit you?"

"I've answered all your questions about Grace. Ask me about the detective."

"Did you kill Detective Barclay?"

"No, I did not."

"Do you know who killed Detective Barclay?"

"No, I do not."

"Are you lying to me?"

"Absolutely not."

Joe let go of Kyle's wrist and looked at Katie. "I hate to say it, but it seems he's telling the truth."

"What? Are you sure?"

"I can't be sure about anything, but his body shows no signs of deception."

"I told you I didn't do it. So, I suggest you go back to that hole you crawled out of and leave me alone."

"You still need to face justice for what you did to Grace," Katie said.

"Justice? I won't get justice. Nobody will believe it was an accident."

"It didn't help that you dumped her body in the river," Joe said. "You should have come forward right away."

"Yes, I should have, but I didn't. I panicked, and I have to live with what I did, but I'm not going to jail for it. Everything you have is circumstantial evidence, and if you push it too far, my father will arrest you or run you out of town."

Katie pointed her finger at Kyle. "Your father may be the police chief, but we know a senator who owes us a favor. You won't win this."

As Katie and Joe walked back to the car, Joe said, "I'm not sure Senator Erickson even likes us."

"Of course, he likes us. We solved his wife's murder and kept him from going to prison."

"We solved his wife's murder with the help of Mayor Ford, a man he despises."

"It doesn't matter. Kyle doesn't know that. I bet he's wetting his pants right now."

After they got in the car, Katie said, "Whatever happens to Kyle, we're still in the same boat. We have no idea who killed David Barclay."

"I think I know who did it," Joe said.

Chapter 14

When they returned to town, they passed a Minaka police cruiser parked alongside the main road just past the welcome sign. Katie glanced at the speedometer, then looked in her rearview mirror, where she saw the cruiser turn on its lights and pull onto the street behind her.

"Uh, oh!" she said.

Joe turned around and saw the police car following them. "Were you speeding?"

"No, I wasn't. It seems Chief Bronson is unhappy that we talked to his son."

"They can't arrest us. We did nothing illegal."

"Welcome to small-town justice, Joe."

Katie turned down a side street and pulled over. The police car parked behind them. Nothing happened for a couple of minutes, and then two officers got out of the vehicle. One approached Katie's side of the car, and the other approached Joe's side. Both officers were young and male, but they looked quite different. One was tall with pasty white skin and blond hair. He was the officer they saw behind the desk when they first visited the police station. The other was of average height with darker skin and short, black hair. Katie remembered seeing both officers but didn't know either one personally.

Katie buzzed her window down as the blond officer approached. She said, "Hi, officer. What is this about? I wasn't speeding."

The officer leaned over, looked inside the car, and said, "Get out of the car. Both of you."

Katie and Joe looked at each other, and then they both got out. "What is this about?" Katie asked again after she stepped outside. "We did nothing wrong."

"Put your hands on the vehicle and spread your legs apart." The officer pointed a finger at Joe. "You, too."

"I protest this treatment," Katie said. "Your chief's son killed Grace Ellington, and he sent you to arrest us because we know too much."

"The two officers looked at each other, and the blond one said, "You can tell it to the judge. Now, do what we ask, or you can add resisting arrest to the charges."

Katie and Joe both leaned against Katie's car while the officers frisked them. They then put them in handcuffs. The blond officer said, "You are under arrest for obstruction of justice, interfering with an investigation, and harassment."

"Oh, c'mon!" Katie said. "You know this is bullshit."

"You have the right to remain silent," the officer continued. "Anything you say can and will be used against you in a court of law. You have the right to an attorney. If you cannot afford an attorney, one will be provided for you. Do you understand these rights, as I've read them to you?"

Katie and Joe both said "yes" before the officers placed them in the back seat of the police cruiser.

"He can't get away with this," Katie said to Joe.

"He's trying to scare us. He wants us to give up the investigation and leave his son alone."

"Yeah. Unfortunately, he's holding all the cards."

"We do have a right to a phone call," Joe said. "You could call the mayor and tell him what we know."

"That's a good idea, Joe, and you can call Emily Anderson."

They parked in the back of the police station, and the officers led Katie and Joe through the rear entrance and up a flight of stairs to the second floor. They then went through the intake process, which included them getting fingerprinted and photographed. When they finished, the officers put them in a small room, no bigger than a bathroom, but without a toilet or sink. It only had a bench at the far end of the room, big enough for two people to sit on. Solid block walls fully enclosed it, except for the door, which resembled a typical jail cell door with iron bars.

"What about our phone call?" Katie asked as the dark-haired officer closed the door.

He looked at the other officer and shrugged. "You'll get your call," he said as he walked away.

"When?" Katie demanded.

Both officers ignored her question and left the room.

A few minutes later, Cheryl came into the room. "I just heard you two were arrested. I'm so sorry this happened to you."

"Your chief is protecting his son. He's the one who killed Grace Ellington and dumped her body in the river."

Cheryl covered her mouth in shock. "Kyle? Are you certain?"

"Yes. He confessed it to us. Now the chief is trying to sweep it under the rug. That's why we're in here."

"Wow! I can't believe the chief would do something like that, although I guess if it were someone in my family accused of a crime, I might look the other way."

"Looking the other way is not the same as having people arrested for knowing too much," Joe said.

"I agree. That's wrong."

"They haven't given us a phone call yet," Katie said. "Do you think you can help us get that, at least?"

Cheryl looked over her shoulder and said, "The chief is pretty pissed right now, but I'll see what I can do."

"Tell him we have a proposition for him," Joe said.

Katie looked at Joe and raised an eyebrow. "Proposition? What Proposition?"

"Trust me, Katie. I have an idea."

"Okay," Cheryl said. "What's your proposition?"

"It's probably better that you stay out of any negotiations," Joe said. "Just tell him we are willing to make a deal."

Katie shook her head. "No, Joe! We are not going to let that man intimidate us."

Joe put his hands on Katie's shoulders and said, "I need you to trust me on this one."

Katie thought for a moment and turned to Cheryl. "Go ahead and tell him."

"Okay," Cheryl said. "We'll see what happens."

About ten minutes later, the chief walked through the door, followed by Ken Daniels and Cheryl Ripley. The chief stepped up to the holding cell door and said, "Okay, what is this proposition you are talking about?"

Joe stepped up to the door and said, "You and I both know you can't legally hold us for very long, so I propose that if you let us go now, Katie and I will leave town today and go back home. After today, you will never hear from us again."

The chief remained silent for several seconds before finally saying, "Do you promise to stay gone and never harass my son again?"

"We can't promise to stay gone, since Katie's parents and friends live here, but we can promise that when we do return, it will be for a social visit and we will not go near your son."

The chief thought for a moment and said, "Okay, fine."

"So we have a deal?" Joe asked, holding his hand through the bars.

"We have a deal," the chief said, shaking Joe's hand.

When they shook hands, Joe connected to the chief. He immediately found his heart muscle and instructed it to relax. "You don't look well," Joe said before the chief collapsed to the ground.

"He's having a heart attack!" Joe yelled. "Let me out! I can help him. I have medical training."

Cheryl looked at Ken and yelled, "Let him out! Let him out!"

Ken fumbled through his keys until he found the right one. He quickly opened the door, and Joe raced out, followed by Katie. Joe knelt and took the chief's wrist in his hand like he was checking for a pulse. He connected to him again and restarted his heart.

At the same time, he instructed his body to quickly release every feel-good hormone that the human body is capable of producing. He gave him chest compressions with one hand while holding his wrist with the other. To an experienced observer, it would have looked like he had no idea what he was doing, but the chief opened his eyes and asked, "What happened?"

"You had a heart attack," Joe said while he continued to instruct his body to release those feel-good hormones.

Joe didn't know the names of each hormone, but he knew what they did. He also knew that in large quantities, he could use them as a potent truth serum.

"A heart attack? That's crazy. I feel great."

Joe helped the chief stand up while continuing to force more hormones into his bloodstream. "Are you feeling good?" Joe asked.

The chief laughed. "I never felt better."

"I'm impressed with how you used your position to protect your son after he killed Grace Ellington," Joe said.

The chief laughed again and shook his head. "That boy is a pain in my ass, but he's all I got, so I have to protect him."

"You recognized your son's ring, didn't you?"

"His mom had that made for him when he started college. She was so proud of him."

"Detective Dave would have figured it out," Joe said.

"It's unfortunate he was too smart for his own good. I liked the guy, but my son must come first, even if he's a huge disappointment sometimes," he said, laughing.

"I know what you mean," Joe said. "I have a son, and I would do anything for him."

"That's right. You have to do what is necessary to protect them," the chief said, now laughing almost uncontrollably.

"Then Mitch Hartney showed up, and you thought he was the perfect patsy."

"He was like a gift from Heaven." The chief held his stomach and straightened his posture. He took a couple of deep breaths and said, "I don't know why I'm laughing. I hated to kill Dave, but I had to do it to protect Kyle. You understand, don't you?"

Ken and Cheryl looked at each other, shocked at the revelation. Joe looked at Ken and said, "Sergeant Daniels, I think you know what you need to do."

174

Ken stepped forward and grabbed the chief's arm. "Chief Bronson, you're under arrest for the murder of Detective Barclay."

After Ken read him his rights and took him away, Cheryl said, "I can't believe the chief was capable of murder."

"I'm sure after his wife died, he felt a great burden of responsibility for his son," Katie said.

"I suppose, but he was the one who mentioned that Dave found a ring at the crime scene. Why would he do that if he was the one who killed Dave and took the ring?"

"I can guess at that one," Katie said. "There were several people at that crime scene, including you. Someone probably saw David find something. If the chief said nothing and someone raised questions about what the detective had found, the chief would have been in hot water for not speaking up. By telling a half-truth, nobody would suspect him."

"It was such a terrible and unnecessary tragedy," Cheryl said.

"Especially because his son will still face charges now for what he did," Katie said. "Although I'm sure he will serve far less time than his father will."

"I guess we're going to need a new chief," Cheryl said. "The one thing I can't understand is how you got a confession out of him. It's like you drugged him, but the officers searched both of you when they brought you in."

"I think when he had the heart attack, the lack of oxygen to his brain must have caused a delirium," Joe said.

"I suppose, but I never heard of anything like that before."

Chapter 15

Katie and Joe decided to stay in Minaka until after Grace's funeral. The following morning, Katie put on her best outfit, and Joe filmed her giving a news report for Channel 23. When she finished, Joe gave her the memory card, and she sent the report to her former boss.

Katie's parents arrived home later that morning with Joey. Katie swept him up in her arms as soon as she saw him. "Oh, Joey. Mommy and Daddy missed you so much."

A short time later, while Joey was napping, they all sat together in the living room. "Mom. Dad," Katie said. "We have been keeping a secret from you, but we think it's time to tell you."

"A secret?" Mary said with a worried expression on her face. "What is it? You're not moving out of state, are you?"

"No, of course not. We love where we are." Katie looked at Joe and back at her parents. "It's more complicated than that."

Joe interrupted, saying, "It's my fault. I made it clear when I met Katie that people knowing could cause problems for me, but we should have told you earlier."

"Don't blame Joe," Katie said. "It's my fault, too."

"What are you getting at?" Karl asked.

Joe looked at Katie and said, "Tell them the story like you told Gabe."

Gabe, a Milwaukee police captain and also their friend, learned that Joe had lied about his identity, so they had to tell him the truth about Joe's healing abilities. It was a secret he faithfully kept.

Katie turned to her parents. "A long time ago, in a small village in northwestern Croatia, there lived men known as Healers."

"I know about the Healers," Mary said. "What do they have to do with anything?"

"You know about the Healers, Mom? But how?"

"Grandma Eva told me. I guess they were a big deal where she came from."

"What did she tell you exactly?" Joe asked.

"She said they could heal people just by touching them."

"Why did you never tell me this?" Katie demanded.

Mary's eyes narrowed. "Why are you upset, Katie. It was only a legend, like Bigfoot or the Loch Ness Monster. I didn't think it was worth repeating."

"It's not a legend, Mom. It's true."

Joe put his hand on Katie's and said, "It's okay, Honey. Finish the story."

Katie looked at her parents, cleared her throat, and continued. "Anyway, during the First World War, the village where the Healers came from was decimated. Most of the male inhabitants were killed, including the last Healer."

"I know all this, Honey."

"Mom, please!"

"Okay, I will listen."

"A young pregnant woman fled the village and managed to get passage on a ship heading to America. The journey was rough, especially for a pregnant woman. She died the day the ship docked in New York, but not before giving birth to a baby boy. That boy was given the name Josip Novak."

Katie's parents both looked surprised. Karl looked at Joe and asked, "Was that a relative of yours?"

Joe shook his head, "Not exactly."

"The boy was adopted and took the name Joe Young," Katie continued. "He didn't know it at first, but he was different from other people. He had inherited the Healer's ability, but he had no idea he could heal anyone but himself. But he could heal himself. In particular, he could heal himself from aging."

"The legend does say that the Healers don't age," Mary said. "Where did you hear this story?"

"I'll get to that," Katie said. "The man married, and the couple had three children. After many years, his wife died at an old age, but he remained young."

"Like the Highlander," Karl said.

"Exactly," Katie said and smiled at Joe. She turned back to her parents. "Back in the early eighties, he faked his death, moved to Wisconsin, and changed his name back to his given name."

Mary and Karl looked at each other but said nothing.

Katie continued. "After his wife died, he became a recluse."

"I don't think 'recluse' is the right word," Joe said.

Katie held up a hand to Joe. "Who's telling this story?"

"Carry on."

"After his wife died, he became a recluse. He spent over twenty years living alone. Eventually, he met a woman who helped him learn about his ancestors and the abilities locked within him. He struggled at first, but when he and that woman were caught in an explosion, he discovered how to use his ability to save her life, almost losing his own in the process."

Mary and Karl looked at each other, shocked. "Wait a minute," Karl said.

Mary interrupted. "Are you saying Joe is a Healer?"

"That's right," Katie said.

"The Healers are a myth," Mary said. "If this is some kind of a joke, I don't think it's funny."

"It's no joke," Joe said. "I can prove it if you will let me."

"Okay. How can you prove it?" Mary asked.

Joe got up and sat next to Mary on the sofa. "Give me your hand," he said.

Mary held up her hand, and Joe held it. "You will feel something unlike anything you have felt before," he said. "Don't worry. It's nothing to fear."

"Okay," she said. "Go ahead."

When Joe connected to Mary, she screamed. "Oh, my God! What is happening?"

"It's okay," Joe said. "It's nothing to worry about. You are feeling yourself and me, from a perspective you're not used to. After a while, it will be like a day at the beach."

"This is amazing, Joe. Do you feel this all the time?"

"Yes, but I was born with this ability, so it feels perfectly normal to me."

"And all this time I thought those stories were just someone's fantasy."

"Concentrate on what you feel, Mary. You have several issues that require attention. Can you feel them?"

"After several seconds, Mary said, "Yes. I feel them. I don't understand how, but I can feel them."

"We can work on fixing those later today when we have time," Joe said and let go of Mary's hand. He then showed Karl what he showed Mary. He was equally impressed.

When Joe returned to his chair, Mary said, "Now I can't help but wonder if Bigfoot and the Loch Ness Monster are real."

"There is one more thing," Katie said. "Little Joey is a Healer, too."

***

The following day, Katie's parents drove to the local funeral home while Katie, Joe, and little Joey sat behind them in the back seat. Katie and Joe didn't pack any of what Joe called "funeral clothes." Fortunately, Katie had the foresight to ask her parents to pick up appropriate clothes for them before they returned to Minaka.

They met Jenna, Mitch, and their two kids in the parking lot. Everyone greeted each other with a hug, and Mitch said, "I will never be able to thank you two enough for what you did for me."

"You just did," Katie said.

They went inside and greeted the mayor, his wife, and their son. The mayor looked at Katie and Joe and said, "We will never be able to bring Grace back, but at least we have some closure thanks to you two."

After the funeral, they returned to Katie's parents' house, changed into casual clothes, and headed home. Katie's mom urged them to stay longer, but Katie said they had work to do at home.

When they got home, it was late, and they were both tired. Joey was sleeping, so Katie put him to bed while Joe retrieved the luggage from the car. They both slumped into the sofa together.

"I think this is a good time for a healing session," Joe said.

"Anytime is a good time for a healing session." Those words had become Katie's standard reply.

Joe held Katie's hand and connected with her. They could both feel everything that was happening inside their bodies. Katie's heart raced when she felt it. The last time, Joe pointed it out to her, but this time she felt it first. "Oh, my God, Joe! Do you feel it?"

After a few seconds, he smiled and said, "Yes, I do. You're pregnant."

I truly appreciate you taking the time to read Last Hope. I hope you enjoyed following Katie and Joe on their latest adventure.

I would be incredibly grateful if you left a review on Amazon, Goodreads, or wherever you purchased this book. Your thoughts help other readers discover the series and mean a lot to me as an author. Whether it's a few words or a detailed review, your feedback makes a difference.

Thank you again for your support. I couldn't do this without readers like you.

Charles Huss

Books by Charles Huss

Last Healer Mysteries Series

Joe, a reclusive, ageless centenarian, meets Katie, an ambitious news personality with dreams of being an investigative reporter. Together, they solve crimes and explore the full potential of Joe's healing abilities while navigating the complexities of their intimate relationship.

Book One - The Last Healer

On the eve of her thirtieth birthday, Katie, a television news reporter, unhappy with her career and her love life, decides to spend the weekend alone at a Wisconsin ski resort.

Joe is a man content to live a private life in his cabin in the woods. Since the death of his wife, he has avoided intimate relationships and prefers to keep a low profile to prevent people from learning of his unusual abilities.

On the way to the ski resort, Katie makes a wrong turn during a snowstorm and hits Joe with her car. Lost and with no cell signal, Katie tries to keep Joe alive until she can get help. During Joe's recovery, Katie learns his secret and soon helps to investigate his family's mysterious past while Joe helps Katie investigate a double murder. Love blossoms while they slowly unravel both mysteries, but danger lies ahead. Can Joe discover the full extent of his abilities before it is too late?

Book Two - Last Rites

In this gripping sequel to "The Last Healer," Katie and Joe, fresh from their honeymoon, must race to Milwaukee to save the life of Katie's dear friend Ashley after she and her mother fall victim to a ruthless attack. With Ashley on the brink of death, while a priest delivers Last Rites, her only chance for survival is Joe's remarkable healing powers.

What starts as a rescue mission turns into a murder investigation as they investigate the killing of Ashley's mother. While searching for the shooter, their investigation leads them to a chilling conspiracy centered on the city's homeless population. As they uncover more of the truth, they become targets as someone is determined to silence them. Will Katie and Joe find who is behind a series of murders, or will they become the next victims?

Book 3 – Last Chance

In Book Three of the Last Healer Mysteries, Katie and Joe, after deciding to quit investigating murders, are thrust back into it when a man is murdered at Joe's resort.

The victim is no ordinary man. He is a suspected jewel thief, believed to have hidden stolen jewels at the resort. While they struggle to handle all the treasure seekers, Katie and Joe debate how involved they should be in the murder investigation. They don't know the killer lurks in the background, taking orders from some of the most powerful people in Wisconsin while he waits for Katie and Joe to find what he is looking for.

Book 4 – Last Flight

In Book Four of the Last Healer Mysteries series, Katie and Joe witness the deadly crash of a prototype aircraft and save the life of one of its occupants. After Joe discovers evidence of sabotage, Katie insists she can investigate the crime despite being almost nine months pregnant.

Someone planted an explosive device in the aircraft, killing the company's founder and jeopardizing the struggling startup's future. Was the attack meant to destroy the company, or was it something more personal? As Katie and Joe hit one dead end after another, they discover the killer isn't finished. With time running out, they race to save the next victim, but with people dying, a murderer on the loose, and Katie in labor, what's a Healer to do?

Book 5 – Last Hope

In the fifth Last Healer Mystery, Katie and Joe learn of a tragedy in Katie's hometown while they are celebrating their son's first birthday. The husband of Katie's childhood best friend stands accused of murdering the town's lone detective. They return to the small Wisconsin town, determined to find the real killer.

As they dig deeper, they uncover chilling ties between the detective's death and the recent killing of the mayor's daughter. It soon becomes clear someone will stop at nothing to keep the truth buried.

Other Books by Charles Huss

Truth Be Told

Peter Beckett awoke 25 years ago with no memory of his past. Since then, he's been haunted by a gift he never asked for and doesn't want. People can't lie to him. To Peter, it feels like a curse that has left him isolated and feared by all who get to know him. Only his priest accepts him for who he is.

The FBI has been watching him, and they need his unique talent to track a deadly drug cartel that has infiltrated Milwaukee, fueling a dangerous spike of fentanyl overdoses. Rookie agent Hannah Meyers is assigned to recruit Peter, who is reluctant to help, but is intrigued by Hannah after she lies to him.

As the investigation deepens, details of Peter's former life emerge. With secrets unraveling and lives on the line, Peter must decide whether to return to the glorious life he once knew or give it all up for love.

Saving Apollo

Apollo is no ordinary dog. Along with his sister, Athena, he was genetically modified to be smarter than a chimpanzee. When the lead geneticist quits over a dispute about the fate of the dogs, chaos erupts, and Apollo escapes, ending up on a small island off the Florida coast. There, he befriends twelve-year-old Ethan, who has just moved to the island with his dad, Ryan.

As they uncover Apollo's extraordinary ability to understand them, they also learn about the perilous fate that awaits him if he returns. With the help of their neighbor, Brooke, a local veterinarian, they devise a plan to save Apollo and Athena. Standing in their way is Jack Strauss, a former Marine and head of security at the lab that created Apollo and Athena.

"Saving Apollo" is a heartwarming, family-friendly story of friendship, love, and compassion.

Falling Star

A meteorite crashes into the serene wilderness of a national park. In its aftermath, both people and animals succumb to aggressive behavior followed by death. Two rookies, FBI agent Beth Hartley and Park Ranger Mike Bauer, are put together to investigate the strange events.

Beth is tough as they come on the outside, but vulnerable on the inside. After her last breakup, she has given up on men to focus on her career. Mike, a former military police officer, has developed trust issues and prefers his new career, where he has no partner to rely on.

As their investigation brings them closer to the truth, they find themselves getting closer to each other. In a dangerous forest where every animal is a potential threat, and even the air could be toxic, their best chance for survival is a partner they can trust.

Identity Crisis

After Alex Neumann agrees to participate in his father's groundbreaking memory recording experiment, he awakens years later to find he is not the man he used to be. He soon becomes a pawn in a deadly scheme involving a ruthless businessman, an Army general, and the President of The United States.

As Alex peels away layers of deception, his true identity slowly emerges, along with skills foreign to his old self. He will need all those skills and the help of friends he meets along the way to survive and turn the tables on his adversaries.

Bad Cat Chris: The Baddest Cat You'll Ever Love

When Chuck volunteered to help a local cat shelter clean cages one morning, the last thing he expected was a kitten climbing up his back to perch on his shoulders, but that was the beginning of a relationship that would test the limits of human endurance and compassion.

This is the story of Chris, a cat like no other who would turn the lives of Chuck and Rose upside-down while eventually showing them that bad can be good and love can come from the most unlikely places.

This book is based on Chris's blog at BadCatChris.com and is a collection of sometimes serious but mostly humorous stories about the ups and downs of living with a bad cat.

About The Author

Charles Huss was born and raised in the suburbs of Chicago but has lived most of his adult life in the Tampa Bay, Florida, area. He is a St. Petersburg College graduate and the author of several books. He currently lives with his wife, Rose, and their two cats.

www.ingramcontent.com/pod-product-compliance
Lightning Source LLC
Chambersburg PA
CBHW030223180626
46810CB00008B/2940